Return to the Hunt

Hugh McCracken

BeWrite Books, UK
www.bewrite.net

Published internationally by BeWrite Books, UK.
363 Badminton Road, Nibley, Bristol. BS37 5JF.

© Hugh McCracken 2003

British Library Cataloguing in Publication Data.
A catalogue record for this book is available from the British Library

ISBN 1-904224-52-0

Digitally produced by BeWrite Books, UK.

**Also available in eBook and CD-ROM formats
from www.bewrite.net**

Exclusive Cover by Alan Geldard © 2003

In the past ...

On the morning of the Hunt the human quarry is let go, one at a time. At high noon, the Duke and the hunters set out. The Hunt lasts till noon the next day. The Rules? Anyone who survives goes free and pardoned. The others die during the Hunt or are caught and executed.

In the present ...

"I wish we'd never come back." Davey scuffed his foot in the dust and threw his empty Coke can in the general direction of the trash bin. "Okay, okay." He scowled at the policeman who had stopped to stare at him, picked up the litter, and deposited it properly. "See what I mean, Pete? Here, we're only kids again."

Some of the pals thrown through a time shift to savage Medieval times survived the Hunt and returned to the present day. After living through their worst nightmares, they now have to relearn how to survive in the twenty first century.

Hugh McCracken was born in Glasgow, Scotland and had his early education interrupted by evacuation during World War II. After taking a degree in Chemistry and Mathematics at St Andrews University, he worked as a Chemical Engineer before becoming a teacher.

He, his wife Lyn, and son David, relocated to Canada in 1967 where his second son, Iain, was born. Hugh and Lyn now live in Ottawa to be close to both sons, daughter-in-law, and three grandchildren.

For the past ten years Hugh has been a full time author and editor, although he started writing professionally much earlier. Recently he became Associate Editor with BeWrite Books.

Some of his short stories and poems may be seen at www.bewrite.net.

Other McCracken adventure novels, especially for his young adult audience (and their parents) and published in eBook, CD and paperback by BeWrite Books are ...

The Time Drum
Rules of the Hunt
Ring of Stone
Grandfather and the Ghost

Coming Soon: Masters of the Hunt

(Digital versions of Time Drum are available under the title 'Kevin and the Time Drum' from: www.electricebookpublishing.com)

A Time Check From Hugh McCracken

The ribbon of time is endless, but do we travel only on one side with our past, our present, our future; our before, our now, our after? Unable, forbidden to cross over the edge?

What is on the other side? Another time line? An alternate universe? Could we get from our time, our universe to the other without crossing an edge? If we did, could we get back?

The Möbius Loop – a simple loop of ribbon with a single twist discovered by the 19th Century German mathematician and astronomer August Ferdinand Möbius shows us – generations before Star Wars – how we might easily pass from one side of reality to the another.

Puzzled?

… try this …

🜂Take yesterday's newspaper and a pair of scissors and cut yourself a long strip, maybe one foot long by a couple of inches wide.

🜂Make a hoop but don't fix the ends to each other yet.

🜂With us so far?

🜂Now … make a single twist in the paper and join the ends with tape or a staple.

🜂Doesn't look much does it?

🜂Mark a cross with a felt-tipped pen on one side of the paper and a circle on the other side directly opposite.

🜂Hold it in one hand, then gently run the forefinger of your other on the inside of the loop …

🜂Notice anything strange? Of course you do! Your finger stroked the 'inside' AND the 'outside' of the Möbius Loop without crossing an edge – you got from the cross to the circle without going over the edge.

⏳You have just proven to yourself that you can traverse dimensions, that our idea of space and time might be ... well ... out of the loop.

This is how your friends in my books might be shifted through the centuries. A simple twist in time and space. Before you tried your experiment, you may have thought this sheer science fiction ... but what do you think now that you are dangling the evidence in your hand? Show your folks, show your friends – see what they think of your first REAL adventure into the ultimate paradox!

Your friend – Hugh McCracken

To the generations of students, and some adults, who perhaps unwittingly,
provided inspirations for the characters in this book

Return from the Hunt

One

"I wish we'd never come back." Davey scuffed his foot in the dust and threw his empty Coke can in the general direction of the trash bin. "Okay, okay." He scowled at the policeman who had stopped to stare at him, picked up the litter, and deposited it properly. "See what I mean, Pete? Here, we're only kids again."

"Clean your shoes," I said, tugging at my clothes. "Your mom'll chew us out if we're messy for the interview at school."

Davey sighed and stood on one foot to rub one toe-cap up and down the back of the other trouser leg and peered down at the result. "I'll be fourteen next birthday…"

I laughed. "You were only thirteen three months ago."

"It's not right. If we'd stayed, we'd be hunting, or fishing, not being dragged off to see some stuck-up old geezer about a stupid school."

Uncle Alex was monosyllabic when we walked with him and Aunt Jean to the school after lunch.

"Mr Lamont, Mrs Lamont, boys. Come in, please." The man behind the desk didn't get up. He peered at us over half-spectacles perched on the end of his nose. "Sit."

I half expected to see a dog. There were only two chairs. Davey and I stood beside Aunt Jean and Uncle Alex.

11

"Don't fidget, boys. Now what can I do for you? I'm very busy."

Uncle Alex cleared his throat. "Mr Taylor, Davey, and my nephew Peter, Peter Macdonald–"

"Ah, yes." The headmaster studied Davey and me over the top of his spectacles again. "Oh, yes. Your son…" He glanced at the papers on the desk. "Davey was to enter first year last August. Mmm … that's where I shall place him now."

"That puts me back with kids who were a year behind me."

"I didn't ask you to speak, young man." The headmaster frowned and flipped the sheet over. "Your nephew, Peter Macdonald you say. I have no documentation on him at all…"

Not very surprising, you pompous ass. I was only here on holiday last summer when we disappeared. Davey's right, we should have stayed in the past. At least there it didn't matter that Mom and Dad were splitting up, and it was fun, or do I think that only now we're out of it?

"Documents, that's what I need, documents. Where were they last year? Get those files for me and I might reconsider. In the meantime, Macdonald will go into second year secondary, a year below his age group, but appropriate if he too missed a year. Now…" The headmaster stood, and more or less forced the Lamonts to do so also, and walked over to the door. "Good day, Mr Lamont, Mrs Lamont." He held the door open.

We walked out of the school, silent until we reached the front door. Uncle Alex's face was flushed, his fists clenched. "Stuffed-shirt, over-educated jackass."

"Not in front of the boys, Alex, please," Aunt Jean said.

"He could at least have pretended to be interested, human. What a waste of time. They won't learn anything useful from him."

Uncle Alex stamped off towards his furniture store.

"Can we go, then?" Davey said.

"Home and into street clothes first. Let's keep your school stuff reasonable for a day or two at least."

We changed quickly and went first to Mike's house, where Mrs Buchanan told us he was at his father's shop.

The photographer's shop was empty when Davey and I entered. The door bell rang and Mike's dad bustled out of the back room.

"Oh, it's only you two. Michael, it's Peter and Davey. You can leave that stuff, if you like, if you want to go out."

"What happened to you two at school?" Mike asked. "Taylor won't let me into fourth year academic stream, just because, so he says, the boarding school Dad sent me to 'is better known for its outward bound program than for academics'. "

"And he doesn't have any records from where you were last year," I said.

"I can either go back to third year or into fourth year technical. Dad really lost his cool."

"What's all this about third and fourth year and so on?"

"Oh, I forgot you're a Yank," Mike said.

"Let's not start that over. Just tell me."

"Elementary is the first seven years at school. First year secondary is the start of high school, about twelve."

"Okay, by age, grade seven with us."

"What year, grade, would you be?" Mike said.

"Into grade eight – second year here, this coming year."

"But that's the same as I should be," Davey said, "and you're nearly two years older than me."

"Yeah, but with a September birthday I missed the cut-off to start school the year I turned six and I was ill a lot and lost another year."

The three of us drifted down to the harbour, then back to the castle, where we lounged in the public park outside the moat. No one suggested we should actually pay to enter the castle itself.

"Remember how grand it was," Davey said, "when we visited the Duke..."

Less than four months ago, or eight and a half centuries ago, the three of us walked across the drawbridge and into the castle to face the Duke. Funny, every now and then I think I can almost hear him, not simply a replay of something from before, but right now in my head.

"Whit hae we here? The three mystery loons?" a voice said.

Three boys about Mike's size grinned at us. One pushed Davey, who, slighter and smaller, slid back towards the moat.

"Davey Lamont," he said. "Ye're no as beefy as ye were. Still cry as easy? Maybe a wee bit catch-up session ahin' the coal shed?"

"Beat it, Ted." Mike scowled. "We're not the patsies we once were."

Ted gave Davey another push and turned to Mike.

"Ur ye wantin' a doin', Buchanan? I hivenae had the pleasure fur whit – three years? Join the queue. Ah'll get round to ye."

Mike stepped forward and with the flat of his hand pushed Ted, who sprawled backwards over Davey who had crouched behind him. When a second boy moved, I stepped forward and kicked him hard under the knee and raked my shoe down his shin to stamp hard on the instep. He bent forward and his nose, on its way down, met my knee on its way back up.

Mike's toe flicked an ankle, and the third boy, about to run away, tumbled onto his face, feet tangled. I leapt on him, grabbed the hair on the back of his head, pulled sharply up, then let go. The boy's nose crashed to the hard path.

"Ow. Ma nose."

I looked round. Mike was astride Ted, with his arms pinned above his head.

"Let him go, Pete," Mike said, and climbed off Ted. "Beat it, Ted. That's it. Don't mess with us."

The other two ran. Ted explored the back of his head with his fingers.

"Ah'll fix ye, Davey Lamont. Jist see if Ah dinnae."

"You do and it'll be your last act." Mike advanced, fists clenched, and Ted backed away then ran.

As Ted and his friends sped off, Davey grinned. "The Battle of the Smithy all over again. It begins to feel more like home."

"Who were those turkeys we just plucked?" I said.

"Oh, yeah," Davey said, "Ted was off-island when you were here in the summer. That's Ted Campbell. He used to bully me."

"And everybody else," Mike said.

"He'd make appointments with kids," Davey said. "Sometimes he'd turn up, sometimes he wouldn't, but you'd sure better or it was worse next time."

"Well, after last year, we can handle him. Right, lads?"

"We sure can," Davey said. "Whoops, look at the time. We'll need to run. Mum'll really roast us if we're late."

Grandpa winked at us as we ran in. "Nip upstairs quick, boys, and wash up. Your dad phoned a minute ago, Davey. Your mum took the call. He was all steamed up. Have you two been up to some mischief?"

From our room upstairs we heard the outside door open, then slam shut.

"Davey, Peter, get down here, now!" Uncle Alex shouted. We clattered down the stairs and turned towards the living room.

"In here," Uncle Alex said from the small room he used as a home office.

"Oh, Oh, trouble. We're for it now," Davey whispered.

Two

Uncle Alex's face was a blotchy red and his cheek twitched.

"Neil Campbell phoned me at the shop. You two and Michael Buchanan attacked his son, Ted. The boy might well have a concussion."

"There's got to be a brain in the skull before rattling it can do any damage."

"I'll have no insolence from you, Peter."

Grandpa came to the door.

"What is it, Alex? You can be heard all over the island."

"These two dolts attacked Neil Campbell's son."

"Whoa. The Campbell boys are all bullies like their father before them. As I recall, Neil Campbell bullied you."

"Davey. Fetch the strop."

"Alex, have you at least asked their side? You know I don't interfere–"

"Then don't. Davey, I'm waiting."

This is silly. Boys our age don't get strapped on the bum, not in modern times.

Davey had already bent over the hard-backed chair.

"Well? Do you need a hand-engraved invitation?"

Uncle Alex scowled at me as Davey straightened, his hands on his backside.

"My dad doesn't do this, Uncle Alex."

"In my house you live by my rules. I'll not have you teach Davey any more disobedience. You can go back to your Aunt Ina Calder's if you like."

I sighed and bent over the chair.

Later, in our bedroom, without supper, I rubbed my bum.

It isn't so much the hurt I mind, though it had hurt, it's the indignity. I'm fourteen – fifteen next month.

"I'll get some ice," Davey said. "It helps if you rub it on."

He had barely opened the door when Aunt Jean appeared. Fingers to lips, she passed in a tray with two glasses of milk and sandwiches. "Grandpa sent this."

This was a plastic bag full of ice cubes.

At two in the morning, I still couldn't sleep. I slipped quietly out of bed, and from the room I shared with Davey, to creep downstairs to the living room. I wasn't surprised to see Grandpa seated in his chair. Grandpa slept little, and spent much of the night at the living room window watching the promenade and the sea.

"Are you all right?" Grandpa said.

"Yeah, thanks for the ice. It helped."

"I'm really sorry. There was nothing I could do. Neil Campbell, Ted's father, still frightens Alex, and many other people on the island. Ted and his brothers are following in Neil's footsteps. Bad news, all of them."

"I can understand that, but it hurt. I've never been strapped before."

Grandpa moved out of his chair to sit beside me on the couch and put his arm round me. "Your back tells a different story. I don't know where you were this last year, but you and Davey have obviously been flogged."

I sighed. *Should I tell him the whole story?* "We went into the wood the night of the closed day, on a dare ... It was weird. Everything changed when we went into the wood, but we didn't know how. Colin died the first night…" Grandpa didn't speak, but sat with an arm round me. "We'd gone back in time till when the castle was new. In a way it was like an adventure camp, I suppose, except the dangers were real. We made some good friends there … The Duke and I agreed one of us had to die the night of the annual hunt. You know, on the night the wood is supposed to be haunted in our time … We killed the Duke, or at least I think we did–"

It's like an itch inside my head, a voice I can't quite hear. No, that's not right, I can hear it, but can't make out what it says.

"Peter? Are you all right? You stopped talking."

"Yes, Grandpa. I'm okay. I think I'll go to bed now. Thanks."

Back in bed, I lay on my back and thought.

It is the Duke's voice I can hear.

I tried the self-hypnosis my mother had taught me. The technique had given me the edge over the Duke before, but it had meant being uncomfortably close, mentally, to him.

"Peter, I have been most confused."

The Duke!

"What time has passed? You did indeed kill me. I remember only the pain of the shaft, then darkness."

I barely slept the rest of the night.

Am I nuts? Would I know if I was? It sure sounds like the Duke. Do I want him in my head? Do I have a choice?

⍺ Three

At breakfast next day, Grandpa wasn't speaking to Uncle Alex. Aunt Jean and Uncle Alex scarcely even looked at each other. Davey ate and chattered as usual.

"What are you two going to be up to today?" Uncle Alex finally said.

"Not much, sir," I said.

Uncle Alex raised his eyebrows and puffed out his cheeks.

"Well, don't get up to any mischief."

"No, sir," I said.

Uncle Alex left for his store, and after we had made our beds, we left for Mike's house.

"If you're headed towards town," Grandpa said, "I'll walk part way with you." He glanced at me, gripped my upper arm and shook me gently. "And don't you dare *sir* me, young man."

I grinned. "No, Grandpa."

He walked between us in silence part of the way before he said: "Have you told Mr Buchanan, Mike's dad, your story? I think perhaps you should."

"Pete, I thought we'd agreed not to tell anybody," Davey said. "How does Grandpa know?"

"Grandpa's not *anybody*, he's Grandpa. I told him last night. I think it was right. We'll talk to Mike. If he agrees, Grandpa, would you be with us when we tell Mike's dad?" Grandpa seemed pleased to be asked and walked jauntily off towards town when we turned up Mike's street.

"We got whacked last night," Davey said when we met Mike.

"What?"

"Paddled, spanked, strapped on the bum–"

"I know that, idiot, but what for?"

Davey grinned. "For ganging up on poor Ted Campbell and clobbering him. Did your dad hear about it?"

"Yes, he'd heard. He laughed."

"Didn't Neil Campbell phone your dad to complain?" I said.

Mike laughed. "You've got to be joking. Neil Campbell won't even come into the chemist's – pharmacy to you, Yank – for a prescription if Dad's in that part of the shop."

"Grandpa says everyone in town is scared of the Campbells."

"When Dad came here first, he'd just retired from the army. He bought the chemist shop and the empty shop next door for a photographer's. Campbell came to see Dad with an offer to protect his windows for a small fee, and Dad threw him out. About a week later, the shop window got broken and Campbell came back to gloat and repeat his offer, at a higher fee."

"Don't stop there you great gowk," Davey said. "What happened then?"

"Dad asked for a couple of days to think it over. The next day, Campbell's old rattle trap of a car somehow started itself and ran off the pier into the sea. The shop window got broken again, and two days later Campbell's boat slipped its mooring and it sank out in the deep channel.

"Campbell came to the shop to see Dad again. He was angry and told Dad he'd been patient and reasonable so far. Dad said so had he. Campbell lost his temper, swung at Dad, and Dad took Campbell to the hospital to have his dislocated shoulder set."

Mike grinned. "Dad sent him flowers; a special bouquet, red and white roses."

Davey guffawed.

"What's so funny in that?" I said.

"Red and white in one bouquet?"

"So?"

"Aw, Pete. Blood and bandages, death. Don't you know anything?"

"It must be a local superstition."

"Anyway, Campbell got the message," Mike said.

"Wow," Davey said, "what a story, but how do you know it? You weren't even born then, were you?"

"No, but a couple of years ago Dad's group had a reunion. They sat up all night talking and drinking. Who could sleep? So I sat on the stairs and listened to their yarns, at least until Mum caught me. I heard the whole story, and some others too."

"If your dad could handle Campbell, why didn't he get Ted off your back? Ted picked on you as much as anyone," Davey said.

"Oh, Mum and Dad rowed about it. Dad said I had to learn to fight my own battles."

"So did you tell him about yesterday?"

"Sure. He slapped my back and gave me a quid."

"Great," Davey said. "We get whacked and you get a pound."

"That's what? About a dollar fifty US? Not much," I said.

"Better than we got. Some ice cream would be nice. Your treat, Mike?"

"I told Grandpa about last year. I hope you don't mind, Mike," I said. "It seemed right. He thinks we should tell your dad."

"Could do, I suppose, but why?"

"Why not? Grandpa thinks it might be useful."

"If you two are through jawing," Davey said, "what about the ice cream?"

We agreed to bring Grandpa to Mr Buchanan's shop in the afternoon. At lunch, Grandpa was quite excited about the prospect and insisted on wearing one of his good suits.

At the photographer's shop, Mike showed us in and locked the door behind us. His dad came through the door from the chemist's shop and locked it. Before Mike could perform the introductions, Grandpa came smartly to attention and said, "Major Buchanan," and Mike's dad grinned and said, "I'm pleased to meet you, Sergeant Major. I've heard a great deal about you."

"I thought you said you didn't know each other?" Davey said.

"We know of each other," Grandpa said. "I was with the Paras at the end of the Second World War. I trained some young men, who later trained and served with the Major. We have mutual friends. Suppose you start, Peter."

"You two wait outside," Mr Buchanan said to Mike and Davey. "Right Peter, Michael said you want to tell us about last year. Let's have it."

I told our story again. This time, I found myself closely questioned. Mike's dad pressed for inconsistencies, and I squirmed, my hands damp, as the questions went on.

Finally, Mr Buchanan said: "You may stay, Peter, while I talk to Davey and Michael, but you may say nothing, right?"

I nodded and slumped in my chair. The afternoon was almost over before Mike's dad said: "I believe you, lads. What you've told us anyway. You're holding some information back I'm sure, but I'm also sure what you have told us is the truth."

Would he, would anyone in this time, believe I could have sent my pain to the Duke? My mind link with him? Do I really believe the Duke is in my head right now?

"Peter." The Duke's voice sounded in my head. "We can use this man. God's Blood, I should have had such a man in my domain."

The world is so far away, like looking through the wrong end of a telescope. I'm in a theatre, way up in the gallery miles from the stage.

"Peter. Peter!" Grandpa's worried face peered at me inches away.

Mr Buchanan, his face blank, studied me.

"Sorry, I was thinking." I shivered and shook myself.

With a last glance at me, Mr Buchanan turned away.

"A drop o' the cratur, Sergeant Major?" he said. "Michael, there are whisky glasses in the cabinet. Get some Coke for yourself and the boys, too. What an adventure. They certainly weren't here last year."

He turned back to us. "Was the Saint Keith we dug up at the monastery your Keith, one of the two youngsters who didn't come back to this time when you did? And the body at the castle your Duke?"

"We think so," I said.

"Your Duke, Peter. That has nice ring to it."

You're not going to pass remarks all the time, are you?

"I've been asleep for a very long time, my son."

⚮ Four

Next morning we loaded up our packs with swim trunks and stuff for lunch, and headed out past the harbour to the far side of town. This close to the end of the tourist season, the swimming pool, repaired in the year we were away, wasn't open till afternoon, so we wandered south from the harbour along the promenade. When we rounded the point, we were in a quieter and more secluded section of the beach and prom. No houses overlooked this stretch directly. We lounged on the grass in the small green which jutted out towards the beach and basked in the late August sun. I lay back, eyes closed, hands behind my head.

What are those two up to now? Can't they relax a while?

I opened my eyes. Ted leered down at me. "Grab 'im."

Two boys jumped me and pinned my arms and legs. Ted kicked my ribs hard, twice.

"No' here," a voice said. "If somebody drives past they'd see us."

"Where then?"

"Across the road tae the auld Logan place."

Hauled to our feet, we were frog-marched across the road and through the gate in the eight-foot high stone wall that ran along the inland side of the road. Ted closed the gate behind us and pulled some dead shrubbery across the gap. Some distance in, we turned off the overgrown path into a sunken area.

The one who had originally suggested the Logan place now scratched his head, shuffled, and said: "Maybe this wisnae such a hot idea. Pa'll kill us if anybody finds oot aboot the stuff here."

"Shut up, Donald," another said. "Wha's tae know? Anyway, we willnae gae in. We'll jist gie them a doing, that's a'. Pa neednae ever know they were here."

"A' right, Murray, if ye say so."

Murray and Donald were young men, older versions of Ted, his brothers obviously.

Our hands tied behind us with our own belts, our feet kicked from under us, we were rolled onto our backs. I lay and looked up at our captors. With Ted and his brothers were two kids about my age and two older young men. One of these kicked at the gravel path.

"This isnae ma bag," he said. "Helpin' ye catch them wis okay, but one's jist a kid. Ah'm aff. We can chat up some girls at the harbour. There are still some holiday people around."

"Me tae," the second said. "Ah'd rather find a bird or hae a beer."

Murray turned his back on them. He emptied one pack onto the ground and smiled. I shivered.

"So, we're no' expected back for denner. Good. That gies us the rest o' the mornin' and a' afternoon," he said. "Like the old days, eh Donald? Remember some o' the tortures we used to try oot on Ted?" Ted squirmed as Murray gripped his ear. "We'll stop in time for ye tae stop cryin' and wash up afore ye gae home."

Without change in expression, Murray drew back his foot and kicked Mike.

"These twa will keep for now. Let's start wi' the kid. Right, Ted, he's a' yers. We'll watch. Let's see if ye need a quick refresher course."

Davey was led off, and Murray came back to stand over me and Mike.

"Ye won't feel much like food, any o' ye, so we'll hae yer sandwiches. It wid be a shame to waste them," Murray said. He turned to me. "Don't ye worry, ye'll get yer turn. We'll come up wi' somethin' special for you. Think aboot it."

Alone, I said: "Are you okay, Mike?"

"Yes. I'll be all right. God, that hurt. See if we can wriggle together back to back and maybe untie our hands."

We did manage to struggle up, but the belts were too tight and shortly Murray and Donald were back.

Murray's toe nudged me. "Should we wait for Ted?"

Donald laughed. "Ah'm sure Ted willnae mind if we borrow him. The gardener's shed?"

I was pulled to my feet and with a parting kick at Mike's ribs, Murray followed Donald and me across the garden.

Murray unlocked the shed door and it opened on well-oiled hinges without a sound. Donald pushed me in and towards a potting bench, the top of which came to my hips.

"When Ah untie yer hauns, assume the position." I stared at Donald. "Lean ower the bench and grab hold o' the other end," Donald said. "Ah hope we willnae hae tae waste time tyin' ye doon, 'cause if we dae, ye'll be sorry."

Murray laughed. "Thae raspberry canes should dae fur starters. Okay, Donald."

Donald untied me and instead of stretching over my head along the bench, I dropped my hands on either side.

"OK, that'll dae. Grab the ledge and haud still," Murray said. "He's done this afore. Been at a posh boardin' school, hae ye? Or one o' Her Majesty's resorts?"

My right hand felt a handle of some sort, and my left, a box of loose sand.

Murray positioned himself to my right and stood, legs slightly spread for balance. He swished a length of cane. Donald was on my left and leered down at me.

I threw a handful of fine sand in Donald's eyes. In my other hand I gripped a small wooden peg mallet, and swept it up as hard as I could, between Murray's spread legs.

Murray dropped. I scrambled round, and hit Donald squarely between the eyes with the mallet. Murray still writhed on the floor, completely folded in on himself. I bent over and tapped him once with the mallet, and he lay still.

When I turned to go, I saw a pruning knife, and froze. I couldn't move a muscle.

"The very thing. We can kill them here and now."

The Duke again!

No. You can't do that in this time. Do you think they're all right?

"I sincerely hope not. This really is a strange time. They behave like mercenaries turned rogue and outlaw, and we cannot finish them while we have the chance?" A sigh. "I am your prisoner."

I could move again.

I pulled Donald's hands above his head on either side of the leg of the table and tied them there.

Murray groaned and twitched as I searched his pockets. I tied his shoelaces together and fled, with the keys from Murray's pocket in my hand.

Mike jumped then grinned when I ran up.

"What happened?" he started when I undid his wrists.

"No time now, Mike, later," I interrupted. "Let's get Davey. Bring our packs."

We crept round the side of the house. Ted and his chums sat with their backs to us. Davey knelt at attention, facing them.

"We will nae beat ye again, while ye stay still like that," Ted laughed, "but if ye move we'll hae a go wi' the cane we found."

One of Ted's chums threw a small stone at Davey.

Davey saw me and his expression changed.

Ted said over his shoulder: "That was quick. Anything wrang?"

He half turned, and I hit him with the mallet on the side of his head. Ted crashed sideways and knocked over one of his chums, while Mike jumped on the other.

I sat astride the one Ted had knocked down and simply waggled the mallet in front of his nose.

"If you know what's good for you, you'll both lie still," I said. "Get up quick, Davey. Did either of these two hurt you?"

Davey peered at the two boys. "Yes, that one, he really twisted my arm. He made me cry."

Mike's fist crashed into the nose indicated and blood spurted.

"Take their shoes and socks, Davey, and throw them into the bush, in different directions. Right, now their jeans and shorts."

When the boys tried to struggle under me and Mike, I simply waggled the mallet again, and Mike pressed on the bloody nose below him.

"We're off now," I said. "Count to a hundred and you can start to hunt for your stuff. I'm sure Ted will be awake soon. Give him our regards. We still have a score to settle, but we don't have time now."

We ran, and took with us the jeans and shorts, which we threw in the first waste bin we passed on the prom.

Davey produced the sandwiches.

"I rescued these," he said, and we all laughed.

"We still have most of the afternoon," Mike said. "What say we go to the swimming pool? We can have a shower and clean up there. There will be plenty of people around."

In the evening, at tea, I broached the idea of a camp out, and to my surprise Uncle Alex agreed immediately, but said it would need to be Thursday and Friday night.

"You'll need Saturday and Sunday to make sure you're all ready for school on Monday."

"Can we go out after tea, sir, to Mike's?" I said, and, permission granted, we ran to Mike's house as soon as we were free.

Mike said his parents had agreed to the camp out, and, as we sat in his room, Mr Buchanan banged on the door and came in.

"I've heard from a friend that Donald and Murray Campbell were seen creeping into town earlier.

"Donald had a huge bruise on his forehead and two black eyes. Murray walked as if his legs didn't want to know each other, and bent over like an old man. Ted was with them, but kept well out of reach. Some of your work?"

We told Mr Buchanan of the events of the day. He insisted Davey should strip and be examined.

"Some nasty bruises, but not all that serious. They didn't try anything else on you did they, Davey?" he said.

"Like what, Mr Buchanan?"

"That's all right then. What about you two? Any damage to report?"

"No, Dad. I've got some bruises on my ribs where Murray kicked me, but Pete looked at them in the shower; they're not all that much."

"Are you three sure you want to camp out?" Mr Buchanan said.

"Yes, we do," I said. "Can you get word in a roundabout way to Ted and his brothers that we'll be camping Thursday and Friday night in the wood southeast of the town? Somewhere behind the big hotel there."

Mr Buchanan looked at me with raised eyebrows before he nodded grimly and smiled. "Yes, if you want me to. I'll also arrange for someone to watch your dad's shop windows for the next few days, Davey, but don't let him know."

"Thanks. If this all works, it shouldn't be needed after this weekend." I said.

"Want me to do something about the Campbells?" Mr Buchanan said.

Mike raised his eyebrows. "You always said…"

Without thinking, I raised my right hand an inch or so and brought it down in a chopping motion. "No, sir. It's our problem. We'll handle it."

"Right, Peter." Mr Buchanan nodded. "It's your problem."

Mike glanced from me to his father and back, a slight frown on his face.

I lay at night unable to sleep and mulled over the day.

"That was interesting today, Peter. Why could we not kill those peasants? You killed my huntsmen, to say nothing of myself."

The Duke really is in my head. I'm not imagining it.

That was different, Your Grace. We were at war, in a sense, and if you'd had a chance you would have killed me. We had agreed one of us would die in the Hunt. Anyway your time was different.

"Peter, could we not be a little less formal? After all, it does seem a little odd to be so formal when we occupy the same mind, and really what could be more intimate than killing me?"

What should I call you, Your Grace?

"My friends and family call me Gerald."

Did you have any friends?

"Oh, that is unkind, Peter. Yes, of course, I had friends."

Why 'Gerald'? I thought you were Duke William.

"Yes, but my name with familiars is Gerald."

All right, Gerald. Why were you so annoyed about Murray and Donald? Was it because for once you were going to be on the receiving end?

"Peter, I am offended."

Total silence.

Gerald, are you there?

No reply.

♂ Five

Davey and I took our sleeping bags and packs round to Mike's home shortly after breakfast on Thursday, and, when Mike and Davey went for some supplies, I called on Mr Buchanan at the photographer's shop.

"Can I talk to you, sir?" I said.

"Would you like some tea or coffee?"

"Coffee please, sir."

"Just instant, I'm afraid. All right?"

I nodded. We sat in the back shop to drink our coffee, comfortable with each other.

"Would you look at the Ordnance Survey map of where we want to camp tonight? That track there." I pointed. "Could you get a car up there?"

"A four wheel drive, yes."

"Can you have someone there from about eleven on? Someone you can really trust? We may want out in a hurry."

"Done."

It was after noon before we were ready to leave. Mrs Buchanan fed us lunch, and Mr Buchanan offered to drive us part way, which Mike and I politely refused. We set out on foot, through town, towards the road which followed the old monastery trail. We were aware we had been seen, and that someone followed us at a distance.

"Good," I said. "Your dad managed to leak word to Ted. Now, without being too obvious, we must make sure they can follow us."

About six miles up the road, we turned east into the forest along a fire break road. Some distance in, I had us stash our sleeping bags and packs and we moved on to explore. I had with me both the topographical and the land-use Ordnance Survey maps of this part of the island, and all of us had orienteering compasses.

"Remember the two cliffs on the Hunt? The one Davey almost fell over, and the one we set the second trap on?" I said.

Davey laughed.

"The one Jamie and I peed over to make the dogs think we'd gone down? Yes, I remember both of them."

"Right, look, here on the map. That's them. They're marked as abandoned quarries. So they come further inland than we remember them, but they're still there. We're here," I pointed. "So we go this way. The map shows the wood grows right to the edge of the quarry top. Exactly like last time, and there's no fence shown."

We found the tops of the quarries. In each case the trees and brush did grow right to the edge of the cliff top. It looked, if anything, more dangerous than we remembered the cliff in the old time. We retrieved our sleeping bags and packs, and set up camp a short distance off the fire break road and within easy running distance of the quarry tops.

"Now, just like the Hunt, we spend the rest of the afternoon making sure we know exactly what is where," I said. "We can't afford to blunder over the top of the cliff. We have to be able to run right up to the edge, then vanish. It'll be dark tonight; there's no moon. I looked that up."

By dusk we were happy all our preparations were made.

"If they come," I said, "when do you think they would try anything, Mike?"

"Not till a good bit after dark. They would want to be able to surprise us, in our sleeping bags if possible."

By eleven o'clock, all was still quiet. The small radio Davey brought sounded loud in the silence of the wood. I heard noises from the fire break trail and flashed my torch once. An answering flash came from where Mike and Davey hid.

"There, dae ye hear that? Ah told ye they'd be along here someplace," came Murray's voice. "There's nae place else for them to gae, unless they gae intae the deep wood. Those saps wouldnae dae that. They dinnae hae the guts or the savvy."

"Ah don' know," Donald said. "They got away frae us afore, didnae they?"

"Luck, pure luck," Murray said. "This time we take nae chances. We tie them up good, hand and foot. Then we take one at a time. Two to hold, one to work. Am Ah ever goin' tae enjoy workin' ower the little Yank who tricked us. We've got a' night. By tomorrow, they'll eat out of our hands. We've tamed tougher kids afore this, have we no', Donald?"

Donald giggled.

Murray, Donald, and Ted crept fairly quietly through the brush towards the sound of the radio.

"There they are. They're in their sleepin' bags, like good little boys. One each then. They willnae be able tae get their arms out. Just sit on them and pound their faces. Now!"

The Campbells pounced, only to find the sleeping bags stuffed, but empty of boys. Mike moved in and floored Ted with a length of branch and shouted: "Run, boys."

Murray and Donald ran after us as we sped off.

"The stupid little buggers are usin' their torches," Donald laughed, as he ran.

Gaining on us, Murray shouted: "Ye're only makin' it harder for yersels. Gie up noo and we'll gae easy on ye."

Davey and I slowed and Murray and Donald sped up. Almost in grasping range, we vanished and Murray and Donald, unable to stop, blundered over the cliff edge. Davey and I pulled ourselves back up to the lip of the cliff on our ropes, and with Mike's help climbed back onto the cliff top. We collected our ropes and checked for any traces of rope marks. Satisfied, we went back to our camp. Ted sat dazed, and shook his head from time to time. We packed up our belongings and checked the site.

"We're getting out before your brothers get back. We gave them the slip. They're off that way," I gestured vaguely. "If I was you I'd clear off. I don't think they'll be very pleased."

We checked our compasses and moved off through the woods. Shortly after midnight we intersected with another fire break trail, and there, half a mile down the trail, was a four wheel drive vehicle.

"Where to, lads?" the driver said cheerily.

"Back to town, please. Close to Mr Buchanan's place," I said.

"Right lads. Hold onto your hats. We're off."

We bumped along till we reached the paved road.

When we passed the fire break road we had used earlier, I said: "This is where you picked us up, if anyone asks. You were driving back to town and we were on the road walking to town."

"Right. Got it. I was on my back to town after a few jars with a mate. You boys looked as if you could do with a hand. All right?" the driver said.

Davey started to explain.

"No offence, lad, but shut up," the driver interrupted. "If the Major or your sergeant here want me to know, they'll tell me. Okay?"

We were soon back in town and the driver stopped at the end of the street Mike lived on.

"End of the line, lads. Everybody out. You can walk from here," the driver said.

"Thanks a lot," I said, "that was a great help."

"Anything to oblige a friend of the Major's, 'bye."

The car roared off down the promenade and we trudged back to Mike's house.

Mike let us in and said: "You two can sleep on the floor in your sleeping bags in my room."

We tiptoed to the stairs. A light came on, and Mr Buchanan appeared. He raised an eyebrow at me.

"We were jumped by someone at our camp, sir. We got a ride into town."

"None of you are hurt? Right, up you go to Michael's room."

Mike was in bed, and Davey and I, stripped to our shorts, were in our sleeping bags, when Mr Buchanan carried in a tray with four mugs on it.

"Cocoa, lads."

While we drank, he had us tell the story. Then he collected the mugs and took mine last, saying in a low voice: "Outside in the hall, now, Peter."

"We have a problem with you boys," Mr Buchanan said. "I don't quarrel with what you've done. God knows, it's justified, but you're like front line soldiers, or special action groups, simply dumped back into civvy street. You're dangerous. You need to be properly debriefed. I may want you to meet with some people I know. They might be able to help. I also want to talk to Davey's grandfather about all this and about you. All right?"

I nodded.

"Off to bed then."

" 'Night, Mr Buchanan," I said.

"What did Dad want?" Mike said.

"I'm too sleepy now," I said, "and Davey is asleep already. Let's talk in the morning. Okay?"

" 'Night, Pete."

" 'Night, Mike."

Six

At the harbour next morning, we hung out and watched the ferries.

"Pssst, old man Campbell." Davey tugged at my sleeve.

An old battered station wagon rolled down the roll-on roll-off ramp onto the ferry. A man about Uncle Alex's age drove. Permanent frown or scowl lines etched his face. Ted peered out the back window on the driver's side.

"Were Donald and Murray in the car too?" I said. "Did anyone notice?"

"I don't think so," Mike said. "There was nobody besides Ted. Why?"

"Let's go to the Logan place. I want to check it out."

The gate we had gone in yesterday looked old and rusted, but it opened smoothly, soundlessly. The path we had been hauled up opened onto an overgrown drive, then to the shell of a big house which had been destroyed by fire. The walls in the local stone still stood, but the doorway and all ground floor windows had been boarded.

"Scout round, lads," I said.

"What are we looking for?" Davey asked.

"A locked door or a window. One that hasn't been boarded over."

We walked round the building and checked.

"Here's one," Mike shouted.

At the back of the house was an old door. Solid wood, one of the original doors that had survived the fire. One of Murray's keys fitted. It swung open on well-oiled hinges. Inside, the floor was flagstone. We were in a passageway about six feet wide. To the right, it led to what must have been the kitchen. From the opening we could see across piles of rubble and roofing to the other side of the building. To the left, the passage ended in another door. Murray's keys fitted this door too. I pushed it open. Inside was pitch black.

"We're not going in there, are we?" Davey said. "It's spooky."

I edged along the wall, groping with one hand for a light switch. A dim blue light came on overhead, showing a stone staircase going down.

A switch at the foot of the stairs lit the cellar.

"Wow, Aladdin's cave."

"More like Ali Baba and the Forty Thieves, Davey," I said. "Don't touch anything."

We walked round the cellar and gawked at the stereos, TVs, and radios, some still in their original packing cases.

"See these, Pete," Davey said, and pointed to crates of liquor; whisky, brandy, gin, rum.

Mike grinned.

"So, Campbell's a fence. The police will be interested in this."

"Tying Campbell into it could be tricky," I said. "Let's check out the gardener's shed too."

I wiped the light switches I'd touched with my T-shirt and locked the doors behind us. There were no tracks on the slab floor and we checked to see we hadn't made any.

At the back of the shed, beyond the potting bench I'd leaned over, were cartons of cigarettes and more booze.

Back on the beach, Mike said: "Well, what now?"

"I need to think," I said. "I want the Campbells tied in, and I want Old Man Campbell to know it's Murray and Donald's fault."

Seven

When we went back to the Buchanan's for lunch, Mrs Buchanan told us Mike's dad wanted us to meet him at the shop. "I've made some sandwiches for you to take. Dad can make coffee or tea for himself at the shop."

I told Mike and Davey what Mr Buchanan had said the night before, and we speculated about what might have happened to the Campbells. At the shop Mr Buchanan waved us through to the back room while he finished with a customer. Grandpa was already there, seated, coffee cup in his hand.

"Have you told them?" Mr Buchanan said when he came in.

"No. Not yet, Major."

"Ted Campbell was found this morning on one of the fire break roads in the southeast," Mr Buchanan said. "The forestry men took him home. He told them he and his brothers had gone out to hunt rabbits the night before and he had somehow become separated. He had spent the night looking for them. Some rock scramblers found Murray and Donald in the southern-most of the two old quarries. Donald has a broken leg. Murray has a broken ankle and the hospital is checking him for concussion."

Mr Buchanan had watched us carefully as he spoke. He had paused before he told us of Donald and Murray's injuries, and as he did tell us, he watched me particularly.

My grin froze on my face. Mr Buchanan shook his head.

"Michael, there are sheets of paper and pencils on the bench in the darkroom. Give a piece to each of you and a pencil. Each of you write out: the objectives of last night's exercises; were the goals achieved; could they have been achieved in any other way; did your operation have any unforeseen results; if so, should you have anticipated what happened; if you had to do it again, what would you do differently, if anything; how do you feel about the results?

"Don't talk to each other about it. Just get on."

He sat for a short time and studied each in turn, then sighed.

"May I speak to you outside for a moment, Sergeant Major?"

Grandpa nodded, and they went out to the front shop.

I sat and thought.

In my mind the Duke said: *"I like this man. There was no emotion in his recital, only the facts. With him and you boys, we could take the kingdom and hold it. Tell me, you would not let me kill those unpleasant peasants the day before yesterday, but you set a trap to kill them last night. Was it simply better fun? Or am I missing some information or some knowledge of today's customs?"*

I put my head down on the table and started to cry. Mr Buchanan came in almost immediately, and waved Davey and Michael out, but thrust their papers into their hands. "Take these with you and finish them, but go with Mr Lamont now."

Across the table from me, Mr Buchanan simply sat and watched as I cried.

When the sobs eased Mr Buchanan snapped: "Right. Sit up. Wipe your eyes. Blow your nose. Sit up straight when I talk to you."

I pulled myself upright and wiped my eyes.

"How many men have you killed?"

I gulped. "One for sure, the Duke. Four others maybe, by accident."

"Right, for each; where, when, how, and why." I described the traps at the cliffs for the Hunt, the death of the Duke and the Huntmaster.

"That's where, when, and how. In each case why."

After a period of thought, I said: "The huntsmen at the Hunt, to avoid capture and death in the Hunt; the Duke, because it was him or us."

"You are sure of that? What is to say you are worthier than the Duke to live?"

"Yes!" I shouted. "It was him or me, that was our agreement, and everyone said he was evil and we were right to kill him."

"Yes, Peter, it was him or you – you, Peter," Mr Buchanan said. "Everyone said – the Duke, his wife, his friends, his son, his supporters? What do you say?"

I wept again. "Yes! When it came right down to it, I wanted to live!"

"Right. Hold that thought. It was your decision, not someone else's. No one else shares the blame, or the credit, no one can judge you, or forgive you, except you. Now, the Campbells?"

"I really don't know if any of the huntsmen died at the cliffs. They might have. Last night I had us set the trap, and bait it, because I wanted the Campbells off our backs. I didn't set out to kill them. I suppose I did know at the back of my mind they might be killed … I didn't much care."

"You could have reported them to the police."

"No! Everyone says the Campbells always slide out of tricky situations. You didn't sit back and wait, you fought them, didn't you?"

" 'Everyone says' again. Who says, what evidence? Yes, I fought back; property for property, only enough force to protect myself, never excessive force, never entrapment."

"I thought I had enough evidence to act. They were still out and free, everyone was frightened of them – all right, I thought everyone seemed scared of them. They wanted us spooked enough to do whatever they said … they would make slaves of us, have us do all sorts of stuff. They were too big and strong for us to fight any other way. What's excessive force? They really did for themselves, we didn't ask for them to come after us."

"No? You had me spread the word of where you would be that night. You set the three of you up as bait, and I was stupid enough to go along."

"With the Duke, it was like winning a game. I didn't really think I had actually killed him till much later, after we got here, to this time. Then I felt sorry for him, but pleased we had survived. I'm all mixed up about that.

"With the Campbells, I don't think I let myself consider the possibility they might be killed, when I set up the trap. When you told us about Murray's concussion and that he might die, my first thought was, 'Good, he won't bother us again,' then suddenly, I felt sick: 'I did it, I killed him.'

"If I had wanted to kill them, I could have done it in the gardener's shed with the pruning knife, when they were out cold. The Duke wanted to."

"Why didn't you? What stopped you? The fact that doing it there and then you would be almost sure to be caught and punished?"

I wept again.

"I couldn't kill them then in cold blood. In the wood it was different. They didn't have to come after us. They had that choice."

"Had you told them what the choice was? Was it more sporting, better fun in the wood?"

"Oh Lord. That was what the Duke asked. Was our ambush like his Hunt?"

"You could have set a different type of trap: ropes, net, a pit. All those have less potential to kill. They would have been

41

trapped, caught, embarrassed, exposed, open to ridicule. All consequences that are very effective against bullies, who rely to some extent on the consent of their victims, who try for peace at all cost."

"Yeah," I said. "I suppose we could, but the quarries were there already. I thought it had to either hurt them badly or scare them enough to make them leave us alone."

"Finally," Mr Buchanan said, "are you proud of yourself? Is this an adventure you will boast about?"

"No!" I sobbed. "Damn you, I'm not proud of it."

"Would you do it again with equally little thought?"

"No ... yes ... well, if I had to, yes, I would do it again to protect Davey and myself, but I might want to think it through more. We could have survived a beating. The Campbells didn't intend to kill us. We could have come up with a less drastic but effective trap."

I blew my nose, more or less cried out.

"Peter, I'm sorry if I seemed rough on you, but you were a boy, a child, forced into decisions under which many men have cracked. I had to be sure. I blame myself. I should have realised, after your experiences last year, what your reaction might be, exactly how violent you three could be."

Mr Buchanan paused. "Those who kill randomly, or thoughtlessly without emotion, and those who enjoy the deed must be weeded out. There is simply no place for them, especially in any set-up in which bloodshed may be necessary.

"I want you to accept responsibility for yourself and your actions. We all make mistakes. Accept that, but learn from them. Recognise them, know what the mistake was and how it happened, how it can be avoided in the future. Now you've laid it all out for yourself, and examined the mistake and your conscience dispassionately, drop it, it is past. Don't keep going back to it like a tongue to a rotten tooth. Store and use the lesson, but drop the excess baggage of what might have been. Our past is beyond our reach."

Mr Buchanan rose and moved round the table to hug me. "Peter, you'll be fine. You three, you, Davey, and Michael, make a great team. I pounced on you because you are the leader, whether you know it or not. I'm finished with you now. Sorry about the sermon. I have to debrief Michael and Davey. We'll meet after tea, including Mr Lamont. Send Davey in, please. He should be outside with Mr Lamont."

"Right, Mr Buchanan."

Eight

I decided not to stay with Grandpa and Mike, but instead walked out onto the harbour. Seated on a bollard, I looked out to sea and thought of what Mr Buchanan had said.

I did feel better having thought events through on his scheme. The same sort of relief I used to find followed confession and absolution. As a younger boy, I had often wondered how boys whose religion, or parental background, did not include the confessional managed. How could they keep their sins bottled up without exploding? What Mr Buchanan had done was like lancing a boil; painful, hurtful, and messy at the time, but necessary, and if properly done, a relief.

I jumped as a hand touched my shoulder.

"Whoa, it's only me, Peter. Grandpa. I've sent Davey for some ice cream for us. Mr Buchanan's finished with Davey, and Michael's with his dad.

"Your Aunt Jean got a letter today from your mother. The sweetness and light of the phone calls when you got back hasn't lasted. Apparently, your father won't agree to a divorce – against his religion. There will be a battle for your custody, I'm afraid. Your dad wants you to stay with his sister till it's settled. Your mum says it's up to you."

"I like Aunt Jean better than Aunt Ina, Dad's sister, but I like Uncle John better than Uncle Alex. I want to stay with you and Davey. Can I?"

"I don't know. If it were up to me I'd say, yes, but you know I'm Alex's father and therefore not a blood relative of yours. I'd have no standing in court. I suppose it's up to Alex and Jean and to your parents' lawyers."

"Don't I have any say?"

"In law, at fourteen or fifteen? I don't know. I think so, but I don't know. Your folks are still in the States, and you're here. I don't know how the law stands. We'll talk to Alex and Jean tomorrow. We could, perhaps, talk to Major Buchanan tonight."

Davey appeared at the end of the pier, accompanied by two dogs. One, an Alsatian, trotted close to his heels and looked up adoringly, the other, a golden retriever, bounced in front of him, and pranced backwards on two hind paws from time to time. Every now and then, Davey performed a pirouette, with a box top high above his head like an acolyte with some sacred artefact.

"Down, dog, down," Davey said. "Get out of the way, dog. You're not getting any."

Davey finally made it to Grandpa and me, and handed the box top to Grandpa. Grandpa handed one of the double nougats to me, took the second himself and passed the third to Davey. The dogs seated themselves, panted and stared at Davey. When Davey took possession of his ice cream, the dogs stood up expectantly.

"Beat it, dogs," Davey said. "This is mine."

The retriever reared up in front of Davey, paws on his shoulders. Davey held his wafer high in the air with one hand and swiped at the dog with the other. He made to step back, only to fall all his length over the Alsatian. Both dogs took off after the flying wafer and in two short snaps it was gone. Davey roared with frustration, indignation and disappointment. The dogs took off at a smart trot, tails wagging furiously. Grandpa and I clung to each other and laughed and laughed.

"Come on, Davey. Up you get," Grandpa said, and pulled Davey to his feet. "Here, you can have my ice cream."

We watched the two dogs go off down the pier. They went on either side of a child in a stroller. The child saw the retriever on one side, and promptly transferred his ice cream cone to the other hand, only to have the Alsatian remove it deftly in one bite. The child shrieked and the mother shouted: "Those damn dogs have just stolen my baby's cone."

Grandpa had to sit down on the bollard – what I would have called a 'short mooring post' when I first came to Scotland.

"They're exactly like you two – a team. One in front to push and one behind. Oh, Davey, you were a picture. It was well worth my ice cream. It's only a pity it wasn't filmed. Nobody will ever believe me."

"Davey, that was great. I really needed it. Fancy being ambushed by a pair of panhandling dogs after all we've been through."

"We've been invited to tea at the Buchanans and you two can overnight there," Grandpa said. "So we'd best make tracks now. Michael and his dad will follow on."

When we walked down the pier towards the shore, a woman brandishing an umbrella bore down on us, a constable panting along behind her.

"There," she shouted, and pointed at Davey, "the boy with the red hair, that's the one who was with the dogs. He brought them onto the pier."

Before anyone could stop her and before the constable could catch up, the woman started to belabour Davey with her umbrella. Davey threw his hands up to protect his head and retreated.

"The dogs aren't mine. They followed me. They stole my wafer," he wailed, and vanished off the edge of the pier. There was a shriek, followed by a splash and a shout. "Help. I can't swim."

I ran for a lifebelt and the policeman prepared to dive in.

One of the local fishermen grabbed the constable's arm and shouted: "Pit yer feet doon, laddie. There's nae mair'n twa or three feet o' water there. The tide's oot."

Davey very shamefacedly stood, water to his waist. He waved at us. "I'll walk back to the shore. I'll meet you at the head of the pier."

He turned. The retriever hit him from behind, and a tawny shape launched itself off the pier to land square on Davey's chest. Davey and the dogs went under in a flurry of white water and oaths. Finally, he made it to the beach. With a final bound at him, and a lick on his face from the retriever, the dogs took off.

Davey dripped, purple with exertion and frustration, swearing like a trooper.

A crowd of interested tourists, lined up for the next ferry, peered down at him from the pier, as Grandpa, the policeman, and the woman of the umbrella bore down on him yet again.

"Are you all right, Davey," Grandpa and I said, as Davey dodged behind us to keep us between him and the woman.

"Oh! I'm sorry, sonny. I wis jist that mad at thae twa dugs. I wis sure they wur yours. Are you okay?" the woman panted.

Warily, Davey nodded and stepped out from behind me.

The constable puffed up. "Are you the boy's father or grandfather?" he said to Grandpa. "Do you want to press charges?" He glared at the woman. "Assault that was. Assault and battery."

Grandpa gasped. "No. Oh, no! Are you all right Davey?"

Davey still kept his distance, but nodded and Grandpa said: "I haven't laughed so much in more than a year. I may have done myself an injury. No, Constable, it's all right. Let's go, boys."

"Have you a change of clothing in your pack, Davey?" Grandpa said. "If so, we'll still go to the Buchanan's. I don't think I could bear to explain this to Alex right now."

We walked along the prom, and Davey squelched beside us, but before we turned up to the Buchanan's there was a sudden splat.

Grandpa and I collapsed on a bench. Davey wiped his forehead and nose.

"Thank God cows don't fly, eh, Davey?" I croaked.

Nine

"What on earth happened to you?" Mrs Buchanan exclaimed when she responded to our knock at the back door.

"Don't ask," Davey groaned, scowling at Grandpa and me.

"We thought we'd better come to the back door," Grandpa said. "We didn't think you'd want the monster of the deeps dripping everywhere."

With a straight face, Mrs Buchanan said: "Davey, you go straight up to the bathroom and strip off. Run a bath. I'll be right up. Mr Lamont, would you like a cup of tea? You and Peter go through to the living room and have a seat while I put the kettle on." She called through to us: "Peter, would you make the tea when the kettle boils? I'll go up to see to Davey."

Grandpa and I still couldn't look at each other without laughing.

"Poor Davey," Grandpa said. "His dignity was affronted."

From upstairs came Mrs Buchanan's voice. "Open this door at once, Davey. Davey Lamont, you hear me? Open up, or I'll break it down and take the damage out of your hide. I'm a nurse. I've seen naked boys before and doubtless will again, bigger boys than you. Right."

The door slammed and the voice was muffled. Shortly after, we heard Davey's giggle.

"Good, you've made the tea," said Mrs Buchanan when she arrived back down. "Would you like a biscuit or a bit of cake? Here, pour me a cup while I get some biscuits."

Seated again she said: "Now, what happened to the loon?"

I laughed. This Scottish word for a boy or young man always struck me as funny.

Mrs Buchanan raised her eyebrows at me, then went on. "He'll be none the worse of his dip, but like Michael, he's very thin and wiry, and he has the same kind of marks on his back."

Grandpa and I described the events at the pier and we were still chuckling over it when Davey, in dry clothes, came down.

"You wouldn't think it so funny if it all happened to you," he said.

Minutes later, Mrs Buchanan's voice sounded from the bathroom upstairs. "Davey Lamont, you get back up here at once. This bathroom looks as if it's been stirred."

Davey stuffed a biscuit in his mouth and fled upstairs as the voice went on. "We don't leave wet dirty clothes in the bathroom in this house, and we clean out the bath. There's half the beach in here."

Davey came back down with his wet clothes, grinned, and snatched another biscuit as he passed.

When Mike and his dad came in, they had to be told about the adventure at the pier, and by this time Davey was prepared to join in the tale and demonstrate his falling around as the dogs cavorted around him. Tea was great fun with much conversation and laughter. The table cleared, we sat round the fire.

Mrs Buchanan scanned our faces. "Right then, who'll tell me? I've had enough of this nonsense about total amnesia for the last year. Michael and Davey have been whipped or flogged. I dare say if I stripped Peter," I backed away, "he'd have the same marks on his back."

"Now, Helen," Mr Buchanan started.

"Don't you 'Now Helen,' me, Murdoch Buchanan," she said. "You know fine I can keep a secret as well as any of you that signed the Act. I'll not have secrets about these boys in this house. It needn't go further, but I will know."

Mr Buchanan smiled. "That's up to the boys, Helen. You know me, I'll not dictate to them in this."

He turned to us. "Mrs Buchanan's a nurse, a psychiatric nurse. She has lots of sound common sense. I rely on her good judgment. I think her advice could be well worth having, but it's up to you. It's your secret, your lives."

I looked from Mike to Davey. After a hesitation, Mike nodded and Davey said: "It'll be difficult to remember who knows and who doesn't, but yes, why not. Can I have another biscuit?"

I took a biscuit too, and chewed on it slowly before I started my story.

Mrs Buchanan did not press for details, but nodded. "I can see why you decided to stick to the story you did. I would certainly stay with it for public consumption. There is more, isn't there?"

Mr Buchanan glanced at me and said: "Yes, I thought so too."

What do you think, Gerald?

"This is a strong, sensible woman. I trust her, and obviously Mr Buchanan does too. She, like my wife, could give good advice but she does need all the facts."

Gerald, would you like to speak directly for yourself?

"Why yes, I would. Can we do that?"

"Peter!" Grandpa's voice sounded very distant. "He's done that twice before, Mrs B."

"Any history of epilepsy? *Petit Mal*?"

I shook myself. "I'm fine. I was thinking. I'm okay, honest. This is a bit difficult to explain."

I stood.

"Your Grace, may I present Mrs Buchanan. Mrs Buchanan, I present His Grace, William, Duke of this Island and the Lands Beyond."

I felt my face go slack, then firm as a different personality took over. They all reacted differently: Grandpa frowned and chewed his lower lip; Mr Buchanan's face was blank, but he tugged at his left ear; Mrs Buchanan had what my mother called her professional face on. Davey, wide eyed, moved behind Grandpa. Mike scowled and clenched his fists. The Duke bowed, approached Mrs Buchanan, and took her right hand in his. He raised it to his lips.

"I am enchanted to meet you formally, madame, although I have, of course, seen you through Peter's eyes. I am most interested to see the principal of a strong chatelaine in support of a strong title holder still exists in this strange time."

I staggered slightly as I took over again, smiled a little lopsidedly, and sat.

"His Grace and I aren't used to this yet. It's the first time we've done it. If you want to talk to the Duke, I'll answer for him. The exchange poops me out more than I expected."

Mrs Buchanan studied me. "Does this frighten you?"

"No. Not really. At first, when we arrived back, I didn't know he was there. Then, he sort of woke up, and I was scared he would try to take me over. In spite of what we thought of him when we were in his time, I don't think he means any harm. We've become friends, of a sort."

"Did you ever hear voices in your head before?"

"No..."

"Have you ever been seen by a psychologist or a psychiatrist?"

"Mom's a psychologist, does that count?"

Mrs Buchanan laughed. "No. Not really. There is a condition called schizophrenia, where sometimes people hear voices that tell them what to do. There have also been cases of multiple personality."

"Do you think I'm sick in the head?" I said. "It's only one voice, and he doesn't tell me what to do. We talk, argue sometimes."

"No, I don't think you're mentally ill. This is an abnormal situation, but I think it's real, strange but real. Your reaction to it and adjustment to it is much more rational and stable than would be true for many. You've done very well. Being able to talk about it will help, I'm sure. However, I'd be very careful who else is told and that goes for all of us."

"I wondered this afternoon," Mr Buchanan said. "You mentioned the Duke twice."

"Wow, Pete. Does he know every single thing you think?" Davey said.

"Oh, Lord, I wouldn't like that." Mike turned bright red.

"At fifteen, I don't think I would have either." Mr Buchanan ruffled Mike's hair.

"Is it really our Duke?"

"Yes, Mike. I'm sure it is."

"Davey Lamont," Mrs Buchanan slapped Davey's wrist, "leave those biscuits be."

"Oh, they're just small," he said.

"Michael, offer them to Mr Lamont and Dad, then move them out of Davey's reach before he eats the lot. Now, what's to do about your schooling, boys? I know Murdoch, I know, 'Don't interfere. They're old enough to make up their own minds.' I'm not interfering. They can't ambush Mr Taylor and a *coup d'état* just isn't on, though with their track record, it's what they might well try. We should try for a civilian solution. Don't you agree, Mr Lamont?"

Grandpa considered for a minute. "Yes, I think Alex and Major Buchanan here going after Mr Taylor, going off half-cocked, might make him dig his heels in even further. I understand he's a stubborn man with little imagination. What exactly are your ideas, boys?"

"I'd like to stay with my own age group," Mike said, "the kids I was with in my last year at school, but I don't want to look stupid either."

"Suppose we agreed to get Michael extra private tuition in Maths and French. Do you think Taylor would agree to fourth year then?" Mrs Buchanan said.

"Oh, Mum. I'd have to work like stink. Anyway, I don't know if he'll even see Dad after last time."

"Murdoch Buchanan, you told me you hadn't agreed, but the meeting was all right. Exactly what did your dad say, Michael?"

"He said Mr Taylor was a rule-bound bureaucrat without an ounce of imagination, and even less intelligence. That, in any properly run organisation, he would have a job more suited to his obvious talents, like cleaning out the latrines."

"Wow, I wish I'd been there," breathed Davey.

"You didn't, Murdoch," said Mrs Buchanan.

"Well, yes, I suppose I did," Mr Buchanan admitted. "I was pretty mad, and patience with fools, diplomacy and tact never were my strong suites."

"And I missed out all the army words," Mike said. "It really was funny when you banged the end of his desk and all those files fell off."

Mrs Buchanan glared and Mr Buchanan smiled faintly and shrugged.

"The Duke says this is like a private family council at home," I said, and everyone laughed.

"I shall go and see Mr Taylor on Monday when the boys start," Mrs Buchanan said, "and try to smooth some ruffled feathers. You, Murdoch Buchanan, will stay out of sight of the school. Perhaps I can persuade Mr Taylor; with a father like you, Murdoch, the poor boy deserves some consideration. Now what about you two?"

"I'd like to be with the kids from my own old elementary class, so I should be in second year," Davey said.

"If I'd been back in the States last year I'd have been in grade seven, that's about the same as first year secondary. Second year secondary would suit me fine."

"Fine," said Mrs Buchanan. "Mr Lamont, would you speak to your daughter-in-law and perhaps the three of us could call on Mr Taylor first thing Monday. We'll see what a little tact and diplomacy can achieve before the gunboats go in again."

Grandpa cleared his throat. "I didn't mean to talk about this right now, but I think I'd better. As Peter knows, his mother and father have separated and his father wants him to live with his father's sister and attend the private Jesuit school on the mainland. His mother would like him to live with her sister, Jean, and attend the local school till they get their affairs settled."

"I don't want to stay with Aunt Ina for the year," I said. "I'd rather stay with Grandpa and Davey."

Grandpa flushed, blew his nose, and cleared his throat. "If your dad's sister, Ina Calder, and her husband John really began to push hard to have you live with them, I think Alex might cave in, although Jean might have some strong words to say on that score."

"That's not fair. It's my life," I said. "I should have some choice about where I stay. If Aunt Ina and Aunt Jean are going to get into a snit about which of them I stay with, can I stay here, Mr Buchanan, Mrs Buchanan?"

"You're the expert in diplomacy, Helen. How do you deal with that?" Mr Buchanan laughed, then after a glance at me, immediately added, "Peter, you are more than welcome to stay with us. My question to Mrs Buchanan was how to resolve this with your aunts."

I dashed out of the room and ran upstairs to Mike's room. When Mrs Buchanan came up I was on my face on Mike's bed. She sat on the edge of the bed and placed a hand on my back.

"It's only me, Michael's mum. Want to talk?"

I struggled up, and sat beside her on the bed, red-eyed.

"Is it my fault?" I said. "All the fights I remember were about me."

"No, Peter. Children often worry about that when parents quarrel or separate. If it hadn't been you, it would have been some other pretext. The hardest part is when you love both parents and want to please both of them still. That sometimes simply isn't possible. Peter, you have to accept the situation as it is. Your parents have fallen out of love with each other. They both still love you, I'm sure. I hope they will be able to keep you out of their battle.

"Can you tell me why you don't want to go back to live with your Aunt Ina? You were with her for the summer when you disappeared, weren't you?"

"Yeah, but it wasn't much fun," I said. "Aunt Ina never had kids. Everything had to be just so. She thought I could go out to play and come back spotless. You should have heard her the day Davey and I went fishing and I smelt of fish when I got back. Uncle John was okay. He played with me, we roughhoused a couple of times, but Aunt Ina told him that he wasn't a blood relative and it was inappropriate for him to do that and anyway, it messed up the house.

"Aunt Jean is different. Davey's the baby of her family. She doesn't let us get away with much, but she knows kids. She's like Mom. Uncle Alex can be funny. He flies off the handle easily, but until he strapped us for the fight with Ted, I got on fine with him. Grandpa – I know he's Davey's Grandpa and not really mine – is great. I can talk to him.

"I've decided. I'm going to the local school, and I'll stay with Aunt Jean and Uncle Alex, if they'll have me. If not, could I please stay here?"

Ten

When Davey and I got home the next day, Aunt Jean told me about my mother's letter to her.

"There's a letter for you too," she said. "It's on your bed."

I ran upstairs to get the letter. I'd spoken to both of them on the phone, of course, but this was the first letter from Mom or Dad since we got back.

Dear Peter,

I am unable to tell you how happy and relieved I am to hear of your safe return. After we spoke on the phone, I cried for joy for hours. Your father and I were frantic with worry when you and the other boys disappeared in the wood. Being so far away made it that much worse.

As you know, your father and I separated November last. I see no possibility of a reconciliation and think divorce is the only answer. Your father will not agree to a divorce for religious reasons, and we are stalemated at present.

We have agreed you should remain on the island in the meantime. Your father will write to you about his views, but I will leave it to you what you do about school.

Aunt Jean is prepared to have you live with her and Uncle Alex.

I think you are old enough to make your own decision about what school you will attend, and who you stay with on the island, but I don't want you embroiled in a battle here, and, as matters are, that is what would happen.

Please write soon, I am dying to hear of your adventure. I hope to be able to make it over for Christmas or the New Year. I miss you very much and have asked Aunt Jean to give you a big hug and kiss for me – I hope you have not grown too old for that.

Love and kisses,
Mom.

I sat for a while, thinking, before I rejoined Davey and Grandpa in the living room.

"Mr and Mrs Buchanan will be here this afternoon, and so will Ina and John Calder," Aunt Jean said. "Uncle Alex is going to leave his shop in charge of his assistant. You're honoured, he doesn't often do that."

The dining room table was set with eight good chairs and two kitchen chairs for the conference. The Buchanans arrived first and Aunt Jean and Mrs Buchanan immediately cornered Grandpa to discuss strategy for their proposed meeting with the headmaster on Monday.

When Uncle John and Aunt Ina Calder arrived, the temperature dropped several degrees. I was puzzled. No one said anything beyond the usual social pleasantries, but the climate of the meeting became wintry.

Uncle John made a beeline for me. "There was a letter for you from your dad, Pete." Uncle John patted his pockets. "I could swear I put it in one of my pockets to bring it. Oh, well. It will turn up. I understand you've had some adventures since last Sunday. You must pop round to see us. We're in the same town, you know."

He put an arm round me and shook me.

"John. It's Peter, not Pete," Aunt Ina said. "The letter is at home. I put it on the mantle. Peter can come for it after Mass tomorrow. You'll come round after High Mass for brunch."

It was a command, rather than an invitation or request. Uncle John nodded at me.

After a slight hesitation, I said: "Thank you, Aunt Ina. Can Davey come too?"

Uncle John promptly said: "Yes."

Aunt Ina and Uncle Alex both said, "No," simultaneously, then glared at each other.

"We have some private family business to discuss," Aunt Ina said.

"Davey is family too. He's my cousin, but I feel he's more like a bro–" I started.

"Peter, one of your less desirable characteristics is your tendency to argue," Aunt Ina interrupted.

"I can certainly sympathise with that viewpoint, or I could in the past. Who is this virago, Peter? We're not going to have too much to do with her, I hope."

I laughed.

Aunt Ina scowled. "I was not aware I had said anything funny."

"Shall we sit at table and have some tea before we talk seriously?" Aunt Jean said.

"Can I help?" Mrs Buchanan said.

"No, it's all right," Aunt Jean said. "Please sit down everyone. The boys will help me."

Davey came in with a plate of biscuits and a plate of cakes, and Mrs Buchanan laughed. "Do you trust Davey with biscuits, Mrs Lamont?"

Aunt Jean flushed. "Jean, please, we needn't be all formal if we're going to battle Mr Taylor together. Did Davey disgrace us, and make a pig of himself at your place?"

"No, no. It's a joke, Jean. A private joke. Isn't it, Davey?" Mrs Buchanan said and put an arm round Davey's waist.

Davey grinned. "Who? Me make a pig of myself, Mum? Never."

Grandpa started to tell the group about Davey's adventure on the pier. The Buchanans, Mike's mom and dad, had, of course, heard the tale, but it was new to Davey's parents, the Lamonts, and to Aunt Ina and Uncle John Calder. Aunt Jean and Uncle John both laughed heartily, but Aunt Ina remained deadpan.

Uncle Alex said: "I heard about it from a customer. From the description, I thought it might be you, Davey. I understand the language was pretty ripe."

Uncle John cut in. "Alex, do you remember, when we were Davey's age or maybe a shade younger? We were fishing, and a huge crab latched onto your big toe. I learnt more swear words in that one session than ever before or after."

Uncle Alex scowled, then laughed. "I'd forgotten that. It was a long time ago. Yes, Davey, it was funny. I laughed when my customer told me, but I got embarrassed when I realised it might be you."

"We are not here to discuss ancient history, or silly schoolboy pranks," Aunt Ina said. "Incidentally, I hear you have been in several fights since your return. Had you been living with me, Peter, I would not have permitted such goings-on."

"I was living with you when I disappeared," I said.

Aunt Ina went pale, then two spots of colour flamed at her cheek bones and her mouth set in a thin red line.

Uncle John spluttered. "And you think he needs the Jesuits."

He laughed, then changed it to a cough. When he attempted to drink some tea and choked on it, Uncle Alex pounded Uncle John's back, his own face red and his lips pressed firmly together.

"When everyone is quite finished," Aunt Ina said. "Peter, I find the change in you very distressing. You were a quiet, devout, obedient child. When you are back with me, I expect you to be as before and I am sure the Brothers at the school will not stand for any of your nonsense."

"I'm not going to live with you, Aunt Ina, and I'm going to the local school," I said.

"She looks like a doll with those two spots of high colour on the cheekbones of her pale white face."

"You will do as I say. I represent your father. He wants you to go to his old school. I hope you are not so far gone that you have forgotten your commandments. Honour thy father."

"Honour thy father *and* thy mother," I said quietly. "Mom says it's up to me where I live, and which school I go to."

Uncle John's face flushed a fiery red, his face twisted, he excused himself, and dashed from the room.

"Peter Macdonald, you will apologise at once. Get your clothes together and come with me now. I don't know what has come over you. The influence of these boys," she waved her hands towards Davey and Mike, "has obviously been very harmful."

"I have nothing to apologise for, Aunt Ina. I will not stay with you, and I will go to the local school."

"Mrs Lamont, you have encouraged this insolence to support your sister. Do you intend to continue to encourage this child, in view of my brother's stated wishes?"

To my surprise, it was Uncle Alex who answered. "Mrs Calder, I appreciate your concern for your brother's wishes, but Peter has two parents; my sister-in-law is the other. I don't know how the law stands, but I respect Peter's right to a voice. He is welcome to remain here with us, and before you start on it, Peter is free to practice his religion here and attend his church as and when he pleases."

I grinned. "Thanks."

"I see no reason to continue this." Aunt Ina snorted. "We are clearly outnumbered and outvoted. We'll call Peter Senior on this, and contact our solicitors. I expect to see you at Mass tomorrow, Peter, and at home for brunch after." She glared round at Uncle John who had come back in. "Come, John, we're going."

She bustled out to the hall, followed by Uncle John, Aunt Jean and me. In the hall, Uncle John caught my arm. "Don't worry Pete. It'll all work out. Coming, Ina, coming."

Eleven

After mass, the priest drew me aside.

Aunt Ina said: "We'll see you back at the house, Peter. Good morning, Father."

"I understand from your aunt," the priest said, "you are to attend school on the mainland, with the Jesuits. Your father's old school, I believe. I am very pleased to hear that."

"No, Father. I'm going to the local school. Most of the other Catholics on the island go there. Why should I be any different?"

"I have seen your father's letter."

"That's more than I have, Father," I said.

"Your father's letter is quite explicit. He intends you to go to St Martin's, and stay with his sister."

"Father, I know what Dad wants, Aunt Ina has told me, but I also know what Mom wants and what I want. Aunt Ina thinks I should be a little plaster saint. I wouldn't be able to breathe in her house now, with all her rules. She thinks I'm still a little boy. She won't accept I'm growing up. I can't pretend a vocation because she thinks it would be nice to have a priest in the family."

"Oh, I don't think that's fair. Your aunt's only thought is of your happiness."

"Then she should let me stay with the Lamonts or the Buchanans, and go to the school here. I can visit her and Uncle

64

John, even spend the odd weekend with them. They'll see me in church every Sunday anyway."

"Think carefully about it. Come and talk to me. I still think you would be better off at school on the mainland and living with a good Catholic family."

"Father, the Lamonts are my family too. I think Aunt Jean feels more for me than Aunt Ina does. May I go now, Father?"

Dismissed, I left the church for Aunt Ina's place. I wasn't really looking forward to the brunch. I was sure I was in for a sermon from her about filial and familial duty.

Uncle John met me at the front door. "I'm glad you could come, Pete. I really missed you while you were away. So did Aunt Ina in her way. She was never off her knees, and I don't know how many candles she burnt. Aunt Ina really means well, but she doesn't know how to deal with people without bossing them." A little more loudly Uncle John said: "Come in, Pete. Come in. Aunt Ina's about ready with the brunch."

Aunt Ina's voice sang out from the kitchen. "It's Peter, not Pete, John. Pete is common."

I went to the kitchen and pecked Aunt Ina on the cheek.

"I hope you wiped your feet properly. The roads are very messy after last night's rain."

I sighed. "Yes, Aunt Ina, I wiped them thoroughly."

"We have a guest coming for brunch, so we'll wait a minute or two for him. Go to the living room with Uncle John."

"Aunt Ina has invited one of the boys from St Martin's. You know, your dad's old school." Uncle John grinned. "You must admit she tries hard."

"You're a Catholic, Uncle John. Where did you go to school?"

"My parents couldn't afford the fees for St Martin's and I wasn't scholar enough to win a free place there. So, I was at the secondary council school here after the parochial elementary school. Alex Lamont and I were classmates, and good chums too, back then. In fact, that's how your mum and dad met. Your Aunt Jean had invited her younger sister to some do or other that Ina and I were at. Ina had invited her brother. I was the one who introduced your dad to your mother. So it's my fault you're here." Uncle John laughed and ruffled my hair. "Being at the local school didn't hurt me. I know the priests would like to have a Catholic secondary school on the island, but there isn't a big enough population to justify it."

The front door bell rang and Aunt Ina hurried out of the kitchen to answer.

"Come in, Robert, you're right on time, my nephew's not long here. Who is this young man?"

"This is my cousin, Tommy, Mrs Calder. I hope you don't mind me bringing him, but he's at St Martin's too. He lives on the mainland, and he's spending a couple of weeks with us before the school opens. We're closed for a week longer than the council schools. Tommy is a year ahead of me; he's going into second year."

"Come on into the living room, boys, and meet my nephew, Peter. He will be at St Martin's too."

Aunt Ina entered the living room, followed by the two boys. When the older boy came in, I gasped. It was one of the two who had been with Ted Campbell at the Logan place. The boy met my eye, flushed and looked away. I stared back. Aunt Ina performed the introductions, oblivious of the atmosphere. Uncle John studied both of us, his eyebrows raised and lips pursed.

Robert said: "Do you two know each other?"

I smiled. "We met last week, but we weren't introduced. Tommy had a slight accident. He had lost his jeans and runners somehow. Did you ever find them?"

"How could you lose your jeans and runners?" Aunt Ina said.

With a sideways glance at me, Tommy said: "Some friends and I were fooling around on the beach. Someone stole the jeans, socks

66

and runners, belonging to two of us. One of the others had to come back into town for jeans for us. We found our socks and runners eventually."

Robert broke in. "That was last Wednesday, Tommy. Ted Campbell came to our house for spare pants for you, but he wouldn't tell me why you needed them."

"What an odd thing. There are some very strange people on the island during the tourist season," Aunt Ina said. "Never mind. Let's hear about St Martin's. Peter will be starting there at the beginning of term. He'll probably be in your class, Tommy, and he'll travel with you on the ferry, Robert."

"I am not going to St Martin's," I said, slowly, clearly, distinctly. "I have already said so. I start at the town high school tomorrow."

Aunt Ina's cheekbones glowed red and her mouth narrowed to a thin red slash.

"Peter, don't be so rude. I specially invited Robert here today to tell you about St Martin's."

"Fine," I interrupted. "Tell away, Robert. I'll listen, but I only wanted it clear, with no misunderstanding, I am not going to St Martin's."

Uncle John had a coughing fit. Robert gamely tried to tell us about the school, but it all fell very flat. Tommy sat mute and ate steadily with his gaze fixed on his plate. When Robert's voice tailed off, Aunt Ina came in with prompting questions, but only succeeded in a good imitation of the Grand Inquisitor encouraging a prisoner on the rack.

She turned her attentions from Robert, who had finally fallen into a red-faced, squirming silence, to Tommy.

"Thanks for the brunch, Mrs Calder," he said. "We've got to be on our way; like the beggars, go when we're fed. Right, Robert? Your folks expect us back soon."

When Robert didn't respond promptly enough, Tommy kicked him hard, and very audibly, under the table, and Robert said: "What? Oh, yes. We must go, thanks a lot, Mrs Calder."

The two boys fled, and didn't reply to my cheery, "See you around, Robert, Tommy. It's a small island."

While Aunt Ina showed Robert and Tommy out, Uncle John and I moved to the living room. Aunt Ina did not join us, but instead went straight to the dining room and very noisily started to clear the table.

"Should I help?" I said.

Uncle John smiled wanly.

"No. Discretion is the better part of valour. We should lie low for now. It's a little like waiting for a volcano to erupt. I told her you wouldn't fall for it. You're too like your mother's father. I remember him well."

"That was fun, Peter. Everyone but us was delightfully uncomfortable. Now we know who he is, shall we hunt Tommy down?"

Shut up, Gerald. Not now.

The assorted bangs and crashes from the dining room and kitchen slowly lessened, then finally stopped. When Aunt Ina entered the living room, she seemed, to me, like one of the illustrations in a primer called 'Martyrs for the Faith'.

I remembered Mom's comment: "If she was like that much of the time, I'm not surprised they finished her off. I'll bet she gave the poor lions indigestion."

The comments had started a row. When Dad heard them, he told Mom they set a poor example for the boy. The memory of the quarrel made me feel sad.

"I see Uncle John has taken you to task. Thank you, John. Now, Peter. That was very rude and ungrateful of you. Robert is the son of one of the ladies on my Flowers and Vestments Committee. I'm sure he would be a very suitable friend for you.

Tommy, his cousin, seemed a very nice boy too. A little shy perhaps, but who wouldn't be, the way you behaved. Much more suitable friends than those two ruffians Buchanan and Lamont."

"May I have my letter now?"

Uncle John began to rise from his chair.

"No, John," Aunt Ina said. "Peter will get his letter when he comes to his senses, and agrees to stay here and go to St Martin's."

"That's not fair or even legal, Ina," Uncle John started, then stopped at Aunt Ina's scowl.

"Aunt Ina, I'll go now. You can keep the letter. I'll write to Dad tonight and explain why I can't answer his letter directly. Tomorrow, I'll get Uncle Alex to have any mail addressed to me redirected to the Lamonts' house. By the time my letter gets to Dad and he replies, it won't be my fault I didn't start at St Martin's."

Uncle John laughed. "As I said before, Ina, are you sure you really want him to learn more from the Jesuits?"

"I was joking," Aunt Ina said and produced the letter from her apron pocket. "Don't be so dramatic and easy to anger."

"The letter has been opened. It's my letter, you had no right to open it."

"Really, Peter. You're so touchy. The letter was from my own baby brother."

"Thank you, Aunt Ina." I pocketed the letter. "It has been a very interesting brunch. I've got go now."

"Think about the school," Aunt Ina said. "There's still time before the end of the week."

"I'll see you sometime next week, Uncle John, or at church next Sunday. Thanks for the brunch, Aunt Ina. 'Bye."

"When you have read your father's letter and had time to think, you'll see I am right," Aunt Ina said at the door.

"Goodbye, Aunt Ina."

Twelve

Aunt Ina's bacon omelette and fresh baked rolls lay like lead in my stomach. At the sea front, I jumped down to the beach, crossed to some rocks and sat screened from the promenade. Blank-eyed, I stared out across the four mile stretch of sea to the mainland, and saw nothing. Finally, I pulled out the letter.

Dear Peter,

It was a real treat to hear your voice when you phoned. My prayers were answered. After your call, I went straight to church and spent most of the night there. I cannot understand where you have been for the last year, but obviously a guardian angel cared for you.

Your mother has left us, temporarily I hope. She will soon come to her senses and return, and we can all be together again. In the meantime, you are to live with my sister Ina, and do as she says. I have phoned the Rector of St Martin's and had your school records sent there. You will be admitted to the school at the start of term.

Aunt Ina will keep you right. Uncle John is a good man and is really fond of you, but he can be very lax in his observances. Follow Aunt Ina's good example. I'm sure with your background as an altar boy, and your good academic background, you will do well at St Martin's. There are still some Brothers at the school who will remember me. Don't be too surprised if some of the Brothers do a double take when they learn you are my son. Many expected me to go into the church. Perhaps I should have. Perhaps you will take the path I didn't follow. Nothing would please Aunt Ina and I more.

I am very uncertain about my future in engineering. I think I may give up the university to teach in one of the good Catholic schools here. Your mother says I am mad even to consider it, but I feel I am called to it. At times, I wonder if I am being punished for marrying outside the church.

Please write soon.

God Bless you,
Dad.

I read the letter twice more.

Didn't Dad want me? Didn't he want me to be happy?

Does Dad count me part of the punishment? If Dad hadn't married Mom, I wouldn't be here. He and Aunt Ina both want to live my life for me.

Angrily, I screwed up the letter, threw it into the receding tide, and watched it bob in the ebb and flow round the rocks.

A shadow fell on me and I jumped up, startled.

"You're Peter Macdonald, Mrs Calder's nephew, aren't you?" the tall man said. "Mind if I join you?"

I nodded warily, then recognised him. It was one of the curates from the church. The one Aunt Ina called the elderly curate.

"I don't mind, Father," I said. "But don't bother trying to persuade me to go to St Martin's, or stay with Aunt Ina. My mind's made up. I've had it up to here," I raised both hands in the air above my head, "with interfering people who think I should do what they want."

The curate laughed. "You recognise me from the church this morning? I'm Charles McIntyre, Charlie to my friends. Relax, I don't intend to try to talk you into anything. I saw you leave your Aunt's. I followed you, because I wanted to talk with you. With you, not *to* or *at* you. Your aunt and I don't see eye to eye about most matters. I got the call later than most, so I've seen more of the world than some of your starry-eyed simpletons. Your aunt terrifies the other two curates. They call her the Dragon Lady in private."

I laughed. "I never thought priests would call parishioners by nicknames somehow, Father."

"Charlie, please. Do your friends call you Pete?"

"Aunt Ina thinks Pete is common."

The curate smiled. "Yes, I expect she would. May I call you Pete?"

"Yes, Father – Charlie."

"I'm a friend of the Major's. He said I should make myself known to you, thought you might need a co-religionist with a slightly broader view than the Dragon Lady."

I told Charlie about the conference on Saturday at the Lamonts' and the disastrous brunch at Aunt Ina's.

Charlie laughed. "Oh, Lord, I would have loved to be a fly on the wall for those meetings. The Dragon Lady must be a sight worth seeing in full flight. John is a saint of sorts. He never complains, even when I see him sometimes in the hotel bar of an evening.

"Pete, can I switch back to being a priest for a minute?"

I nodded a reluctant assent.

"Your aunt is a very devout and well-intentioned lady, but there are ways to God that don't involve wearing a hair shirt all the time. You need to work your way through how you feel about your parents and your aunt. I will listen and help, friend or priest, when you need me.

"Heavens, look at the time. I'm supposed to have tea with some old ladies. If you want to see me, call the rectory. See you, Pete."

Charlie left, at the trot, and I started back for the Lamonts'. Somehow, the sky seemed brighter, the sea less grey, and the people I passed, cheerier.

ᓚ Thirteen

When I got back to Aunt Jean's, Uncle Alex greeted me, but asked no questions. Davey, however, was not so shy.

"How did it go, Pete? Are you still staying with us, and going to school with me? Did you get your letter? What did your dad say?"

"For heaven's sake," Aunt Jean said, "let Peter get in the door and catch his breath. Don't be so nosy. It's none of your business what Peter's dad said in his letter."

"I'll stay on here if I may, Uncle Alex, Aunt Jean?"

"Yes, Peter," Uncle Alex said. "Of course you can. I'm back to Uncle Alex again am I? I was getting used to being *sirred*. What do you call Ina Calder, when you're annoyed with her; 'madam'?"

"I hadn't thought of that, Uncle Alex," I laughed.

"Grandpa," I said. "One of Mr Taylor's problems with me was that he had no school records. All of my records from the States are at St Martin's, the Rector there has them. Dad sent them to him. If there's any problem about the Rector releasing the records, we should call Father McIntyre. Mr Buchanan knows him and he'll help."

"Dad, can Pete and me go out for a while?" Davey said, and at Uncle Alex's nod, "When will tea be, Mum? When should we be back?"

"Not later than five thirty," Aunt Jean said. "And you'll be home this evening. We need to check out all your stuff for school tomorrow."

"Should we go for Mike?" I said as we left the house.

"No, he's out at relatives with his folks. Let's go down to the harbour and see what's doing there."

The harbour was quiet, and after we helped one set of tourists walk their cabin cruiser along the harbour wall to a new berth, we strolled out along the beach of the southern shore. We rounded the bend which took us onto the green on the seafront promontory in front of the Logan place.

"Pete, someone's followed us all the way from town."

"Yes, I know. They've stayed on the prom not far behind us since we left the harbour. It's only one, I think, but it could be more. One on the sea side of the prom to keep an eye on us, with the others out of sight from the beach."

"This is where Ted and his lot jumped us on Wednesday. Just up there on the green," Davey said.

"I remember. Whoever it was has lost sight of us because of the way the green sticks out from the prom. You stay here, tucked in under the overhang. Talk as if we were both still here. I'll go along there to the jetty that's on the other side of the green to sneak a look. If there's more than one, I should be able to see them."

"I'm frightened. I wish Mike was here with us."

"Look, it can't be Ted's brothers, okay? That leaves Ted and the four others: the two about the same age as Ted's brothers went along with Murray and Donald, but remember they left before the real rough stuff started; the two others were the same age as Ted. If they are there, or if they have someone with them, then we simply hightail it back to town along the beach. They won't do anything in such a public place as the harbour. The fact they took the trouble to follow us here shows that. Now, start talking."

Hugged in under the overhang, I worked my way round the promontory on which the green stood to the jetty on the far side. Cautiously, I raised my head till my eyes were level with the green. There was only one boy, on his belly, inching forward to peer over the edge of the overhang, below which Davey chattered. I pulled myself onto the green level, and ran quietly across the green to the prone figure. At the last minute, when I was within a couple of strides of him, the boy became aware of the sounds behind him and started to roll over. He was too late. I pounced. Astride the boy, I grabbed his wrists and forced his arms to the ground beside his head. The boy tried to buck me off, but I rose to my knees and when he fell back, I sat down as heavily as I could on his stomach. By the second repetition he was winded and lay under me, gasping. It was Tommy. The boy who had been at Aunt Ina's for brunch.

"Davey, get up here. It's okay."

Davey scrabbled up the rock face and joined me on the green. Tommy started to struggle and I bounced again, hard, and punched his head.

"Why were you following us?"

Tommy gasped. "Aow, you're as bad as Murray."

"Why were you following us?"

We pulled Tommy over, to lean back against a tree trunk, and squatted in front of him.

"Why did you follow us?" I persisted.

"I saw you leave the harbour. I was stupid enough to think I should thank you for keeping your mouth shut at your aunt's today."

I laughed. "I didn't tell you, Davey. Tommy was one of the boys invited to Aunt Ina's after church today. 'A nice quiet, shy boy,' Aunt Ina called him. I didn't mention it at Aunt Ina's, Tommy, because it's between us. It's got nothing to do with the adults. Call it quits, Davey?"

"No, I think I should get at least a couple of cracks at him on the bum with a stick."

"No, that's enough. Tommy, why didn't you just approach us at the harbour?"

"I don't know. I've discovered it takes a lot more guts to face someone and say you're sorry and that you were wrong, than it did to join Ted in beating up on you lot. I really got a fright when I saw you at your aunt's. You said to leave adults out of it, but I saw you talk to Father McIntyre down on the beach."

"So what," I said. "What had that to do with you? 'The guilty fleeth when no man pursueth'."

"I assumed McIntyre would talk to you about the Campbells and so on. He fairly reamed me out," Gerry said. "No, 'Say three Hail Mary's and a good act of contrition and be a good boy in future,' from McIntyre. He said I had to have the guts to face you, and talk to you. I told him I was scared after the way you beat us, and after what happened to Murray and Donald Campbell. He said, 'Tough; as ye sow, so shall ye reap. I don't think they'll kill you.' Boy, is he tough. Just my luck to get him, and not one of the peaches and cream curates."

"Why not just call out?" I said.

"I wanted to see what the two of you were up to," Tommy said. "I still wasn't sure I wanted to risk a meeting."

"What happened after we left on Wednesday?" I said.

"If you hadn't taken our socks and runners, and jeans and shorts, Harry and I would have been long gone before Ted came round. We'd had enough. You three were more than we'd bargained for. Without our runners, and with our bums hanging out, we wondered how we'd get back into town.

"When Ted came round, Harry got some water to splash on him before he tried to clean himself up. His T-shirt was covered in blood and snot. Ted sat there and shook his head while we told him what had happened.

"After a while, we puzzled over what had happened to Murray and Donald. Ted suggested the gardener's shed. You had shut it behind you, and the door was locked, but we could hear groans and curses from inside. Ted broke a window in the door and we managed to open it. If we hadn't been so scared, Harry and I would have laughed.

"They were both there, hands above their heads, wrists tied with their own belts on the other side of the bench legs. Donald's eyes were shut and you could see exactly where he'd been hit between the eyes. The groans and curses were from Murray. Ted untied Murray and Donald while Harry went for a bucket of cold water. Murray sat there on the floor, dipped Harry's shirt in the cold water and held it to himself. It seemed to help and I think the swelling did go down. Ted and I helped Murray to his feet, but when he stepped forward, he fell flat on his face. His shoelaces were tied together. You should have heard him.

"Harry and I went outside after that, and Ted ran back into town for jeans for Harry and I. We found our runners, and as soon as Ted came back with jeans for us, we took off. I wouldn't have wanted to be Ted that night. I stayed at my aunt's place, indoors, the rest of the day, and all the next day. I didn't want to risk a run-in with either the Campbells or you lot."

Davey grinned, rather nastily I thought, and licked his lips. "Let's take him over to the Logan place, to that garden bit, and give him a taste of his own medicine."

"No, Davey," I said, "we can't. Call it quits. We'd be as bad as the Campbells. Ted beat up on other kids, at least partly, because his brothers beat up on him. It's a vicious circle. We can stop it here or pass it on. You were scared of Ted and thought him a creep. Is that what you want us to be — creeps? We beat the Campbells fair and square. Remember what Mr Buchanan said. 'Know when and why to quit'."

"Honest, that's it," Tommy said. "I'll never get sucked into anything like that again. Honest."

Reluctantly, Davey shrugged. "Well, if you say so, Pete, but I still think he deserves it," then with a grin, "and it might be fun to be on the other end."

"That's it then. All over. All square?" I put out my hand, and after a hesitation Tommy shook it, then held out his hand to Davey.

"I suppose so."

Davey brightened noticeably when Tommy said: "I've got some money, enough for two wafers anyway. We could share?"

When we walked back to town along the prom a puzzled and rather irritated voice sounded in my head.

"God's blood, what was that all about? You had the boy in the palm of your hand. Did you not feel him tremble in anticipation? He is your size, yet he was prepared to submit, and would have done so even if you did not have Davey to back you up. We could have amused ourselves with him for an hour or so, and probably established a binding, lasting domination over him."

That's what Grandpa said about the Campbells. They were on a power kick. Did you hear him? It was the night you were in the huff because I said you were after the same thing as the Campbells. You were and you are.

A sigh. How could a disembodied voice in my own head sigh?

"Peter, how in God's name did we get stuck with each other? I love you, my son, but you are worse than the Abbot in your views on morals. I would have done better with Davey or Mike. Oh well, as I said before, God gave us our relations."

"Pete, wake up, Pete," Davey said. "Are you sleep walking? You haven't said a word all the way back. Here's the ice cream shop. Tommy's gone to buy us wafers."

"No, Davey," Peter said. "I've got money for ours. Here, you go in with Tommy and buy our ice cream."

Minutes later, Davey reappeared with two wafers and handed one to me. Tommy followed him seconds later, also with two wafers.

"Tommy, I told Davey you were only to buy your own," I said.

"Oh, I forgot," Davey rolled his eyes.

"But these were for you two," Tommy said.

"Davey, I could skin you alive," I said. "We're not in the market for a slave, and we'll not intimidate anyone into buying us stuff. Do you hear, Davey? Do you understand? Tommy, I don't know if we can ever be friends, but you don't need to buy us off. Is that clear to both of you? Tommy, eat one yourself."

"And if Peter doesn't want any more, we can share the other," Davey said, and danced back out of my reach.

 **Fourteen**

Next morning, I couldn't eat much breakfast. I was excited at the prospect of school despite myself. Davey, on the other hand, ate his usual hearty breakfast.

"We'll meet Mike, Mum," Davey said, "and go to school with him. Are you and Mrs Buchanan and Grandpa all set to meet with Mr Taylor?"

"Right. Off you go. We'll do what we can with Mr Taylor. See you later."

Close to the school playground, I said: "Is there a girls' school near here too?"

"What do you mean, a girls' school?" Davey said. "This is the school, the one and only secondary school on the island."

"You mean there are girls here too? Actually in our classes? I've never been at school with girls before. Both my schools in the States were boys only schools, like St Martin's on the mainland."

Mike laughed. "The boarding school I was at for two years was all boys. I've had enough of that, thank you."

"I hope you two aren't about to go all soppy on me now," Davey said. "We've had a swell time together this last year."

Once in the playground, I found myself a little at a loss. Mike renewed acquaintances from a year ago, and so did Davey. These were totally different groups, both in age, and simply because Davey and Mike hadn't been close friends before this last year we

81

all spent together. I drifted away from both groups and stood, very much alone and conspicuous.

A voice at my elbow said: "Are you new this year too? It's the pits, isn't it, not knowing anyone and having start all over? We've just moved here. I'm Joan Cameron."

I turned. The girl beside me was about my own height, fair hair, with a hint of red, and clear blue eyes. A total contrast with Margaret, a girl now lost in the past, in the time we had lived through – last year, or eight and a bit centuries ago? Her jet black hair, dark eyes, and bronzed skin contrasted sharply with the white teeth shown when she smiled. I sighed.

"Well, if you don't want to talk to me, I'll move elsewhere, Mr Toffee-nose," Joan said.

"I'm sorry, please, I didn't mean to be rude. I was thinking about something else. I'm Peter Macdonald."

I stuck my hand out. Joan's hand was cool and dry in mine. The way I remembered Margaret's, and I wondered if my hand felt hot and sweaty to her.

"I'll have my hand back now, thank you," Joan said, and tugged away when Mike came up.

"That was fast work," Mike said, "but you'd better save the holding hands for later. We're going in now."

Joan and I both said: "We weren't holding hands," blushed, and stepped apart.

"More fool you then, Pete."

"Thanks a lot, Peter Macdonald. That's what I get for trying to be friendly. Mother warned me about boys like you."

Joan bounced off and left me speechless.

"Come on. Let's not be late for the very first thing." Mike pulled on my arm.

In the school, returning students quickly dispersed to last year's form rooms to be given their new assignments, and new students were collected in the gymnasium. A whole group of children newly promoted from the elementary school were quickly directed to their pre-assigned forms and rooms. That left the *odds and sods*, as the harried teacher in charge of the gym called us, those who were not straight from elementary, and who had not been in this particular secondary school last year.

This left only me, Mike, Davey, three youngsters for first year, Joan, and a boy with orange tipped, spiky hair. He moved close to Joan, and she promptly moved to join me and the others.

"Hi Joan. This is Mike Buchanan and my cousin Davey Lamont. Boys, this is Joan Cameron," I said.

Spiky Hair followed Joan.

"You don't want to bother with wimpy milksops like them." He turned to me. "Hop it lads, don't bother her. She's got a man to look after her."

Wide eyed and innocent, Davey peered round. "Does she? Where? I don't see him."

Spiky Hair flushed and scowled. With clenched fists he moved towards Davey. I stepped between them. "Beat it, ugly. No one asked you to join us. Joan can speak for herself."

We stood toe to toe for an instant. Spiky Hair was an inch or two taller than me and considerably heavier. I didn't flinch or show any sign of backing down by even an eye blink.

The harried teacher bustled back in and the tableau broke.

"I'll deal with you and the red-head kid later," Spiky Hair said quietly.

The three first year youngsters were dispatched quickly. Joan was sent to second year secondary section A and Spiky Hair to section B.

"There's some sort of debate in the headmaster's office about you three, so you're to stay here till a decision is reached. Mr Taylor, himself, will come for you."

We waited nearly half an hour before we spotted Aunt Jean, Mrs Buchanan, and Grandpa leave Taylor's office. Grandpa saw me at the gym door and gave me a thumbs up sign.

A little later Taylor came to the gym. "Buchanan, your mother has put your case very well. I am not an unreasonable man. You may go into the fourth year academic stream, in the meantime. I will personally monitor your progress. Should you fall behind in the slightest, or give any bother, I will transfer you immediately. room twelve, Buchanan. Move.

"Lamont, second year academic, same conditions. Section A, room six. Well, what are you waiting for? Go.

"Macdonald, you present a different problem. A Mrs Calder phoned me at home. She claims to be your legal guardian, and says she has already registered you at St Martin's. The Rector there confirms he has your documents from America. He would place you in second year secondary at St Martin's on the basis of these reports. That being the case I would certainly place you in our academic stream in second year. We lose too many good academic children to private schools like St Martin's. However, I do not wish the school or myself embroiled in any legal tussle over your custody."

"You won't be, sir," I said. "I live with Mr and Mrs Lamont, and I am not going to St Martin's."

"I was not aware I asked you to speak, boy. As I was saying, pending clarification of your situation, I will place you in second year academic. We will be in touch with both the Calders and the Lamonts and with the Regional Education Offices. Section A, room six, Macdonald. Dismiss. Sharply now. Don't dawdle."

I knocked, entered room six, and handed the teacher the slip Taylor had given me. Davey waved.

The teacher sighed. "More paperwork. Do you have your reports with you?" and at my uncomprehending stare, "Sit down there. Here's a blank timetable. Copy down the timetable from the board."

It seemed chaotic to me. Chaotic and confusing. After what seemed like an endless series of instructions, most of which didn't mean much to me, we were dismissed for an extended recess. After that we were to report to our period four classes.

"That's great," Davey said. "We're in the same class, and I'm back with the same mob I was with in elementary."

Spiky Hair was in the other second year academic class, and seemed to have picked up some hangers-on already. One, I noticed, was Harry, the other youngster from Wednesday's battle at the Logan place. The group that emerged with Spiky Hair seemed to be egging him on.

I heard one of them say: "There's a place behind the annex building that's just the job. We can block off the open end, and there are no windows onto it."

Spiky Hair said: "That's them, those two," and pointed at Davey and me.

One boy said: "Like herding sheep. Cut them out of the flock, then herd them to the pen for the slaughter."

At the same time Harry said: "Oh, no. Not them. I'm not messing with them again."

I was not about to let Davey and myself be pushed into a corner where we could be outnumbered, as we had been at the green. No more quiet secluded areas in which we could be beaten at leisure. Without waiting for the usual schoolboy preliminaries of verbal challenges and assorted pushes and shoves, I launched myself at Spiky Hair. It was over before it really started. Spiky Hair was on the ground gasping for breath, unprepared for the surprise attack. I leapt on him, landed with both knees on his solar plexus, and gave one hard punch on the nose. When I rose, Spiky Hair did not stir.

At my, "Who's next," Spiky Hair's erstwhile friends faded, one of them clutched a very red right ear.

"Who is responsible for this?" a voice behind me said.

"I suppose I am, sir," I said.

Spiky Hair groaned, sat up on one elbow, and shook his head.

"Get up, boy," the teacher said. "Go and wash your face. Dust yourself off, then report to me in room four. You," he turned to me, "come with me now."

Fifteen

In the room, I was asked for my explanation, and I shrugged.

"Spiky Hair and his mates were going to push Davey and me into a corner and beat up on us."

"That's not exactly what it seemed like to me," the teacher said. "You seemed pretty much in control. How did you manage that if you didn't attack first?"

"Oh, I did, sir. A pre-emptive strike."

I watched the emotions, the expressions, chase each other across the teacher's face. He glowered at me; a first flush of anger, then simple annoyance, followed by curiosity. "You're not trying to be funny, or impertinent, are you? Go on."

"Sir, bullies depend on the victim being scared enough to co-operate, to let it happen. Sometimes bullies needle and pester the victim until he has to react. Then, when the victim swears at the bully or takes a swing at him, the bully uses that for an excuse to beat up on him. 'It was his fault. He started it. I wouldn't have hit him if he hadn't hit me first.'

"Other times, it's a group. If you let the group get hold of you, you've had it. If it is a group, you pick the leader. He's not always the biggest one. Then you go for him before he expects it. If you're unexpected enough, fast enough, and fierce enough, that often ends it. They leave you be and find easier pickings."

The teacher smiled. "A writer in a poem that is supposed to be a joke once said:

'A Mouse that prayed for Allah's aid
  Blasphemed when no such aid befell:
A Cat, who feasted on that mouse,
  Thought Allah managed vastly well.

Pray not for aid to One who made
  A set of never-changing laws,
But in your need remember well
  He gave you speed, or guile – or claws'."

"That's Chesterton – no Saki, H.H. Munroe," I said.

"Yes, it is Saki, and it seems to sum up what you've said. What's your name? I'm Mr McLeod, I hope you are in my English class."

"Peter, sir. Peter Macdonald."

"Well, Macdonald. This has been most interesting, we must talk again some time. I'll speak to the other boy, but I don't think I'll take any further action."

The door opened and another teacher strode in. "I saw the whole incident. I sent McLean to see Mr Taylor. Mr Taylor wants to see this ruffian now."

Mr McLeod sighed and muttered, barely loud enough for me to hear. "Stupid, interfering busybody." Aloud, he said: "Right Mr Johnston. I'll take him along."

"No, Mr McLeod, it's all right. I'll go with this boy. You can go back to playground duty."

"No thank you, Mr Johnston. I'll report, you take over for me in the playground," Mr McLeod said. Then he muttered: "Maybe next time you'll think twice about sticking your long neb in where it's not wanted.

"Come on, Macdonald, let's face the music."

Mr McLeod put his hand round my neck and shook me gently in the same friendly manner as both Mr Buchanan and Father McIntyre.

Sixteen

In the headmaster's outer office, Spiky Hair McLean was seated at one end, and Davey at the other. When Mr McLeod and I walked in, Davey smiled, but it was not his usual grin. McLean looked ready to turn tail and flee.

"Mr McLeod, this is my cousin Davey Lamont. I live with him. Davey, this is Mr McLeod."

"How do you do, sir," Davey said. "Joan Cameron is in with Mr Taylor."

"Why? What's she supposed to have done?"

"One of his mates," Davey nodded in the direction of McLean, "was about to go for your back. Joan clocked him one with the bag she carries. Wow! You should have heard him."

"How could a girl's bag hurt him much?" I said.

Davey laughed. "She had a wooden pencil case and a full lunch box in it. Right, smack on his ear."

"Why are you here, Davey?"

"Well, the bag didn't knock him off his feet, so I just sort of helped."

Mr McLeod laughed. "Mr Johnston happened to see this from the common room window over his cup of dandelion leaf infusion, no doubt."

Taylor's door opened and Joan emerged. She smiled at me, but before she could speak, Mr Taylor appeared at her heels.

"Lamont, McLean, you can both go now. I don't want to hear anything further about either of you all term. Understand? One squeak, one hint of any other bother, and you'll be dealt with most severely. Joan, you can go too. Most unladylike behaviour. A very poor start in a new school."

I walked into Taylor's office.

"Macdonald, you have not yet been a full day, a full morning even, in this school, and yet here you are in serious trouble. What have you to say for yourself?"

"There was a fight, sir."

"That's it, Macdonald?"

"Sir?"

"I'll have none of your dumb insolence here, boy. Mr Johnston describes a totally unprovoked vicious assault, and your example misled Lamont and Joan Cameron into their misbehaviour."

"Mr Johnston wasn't there. Mr McLeod was. Have you spoken to him yet, sir?"

"Macdonald, you are an impertinent pup. I have sent for Mr Lamont, since that is where you claim to be living. You will wait in the outer office till he arrives."

Taylor walked me to the outer office, where Mr McLeod waited.

"Mr McLeod, can I do something for you?" Taylor said.

"No, Headmaster, but I thought you might wish a first hand, eye witness report before you made up your mind."

"I have sent for Mr Lamont, whom the boy claims is his guardian. I will discuss the situation with him. You may go, Mr McLeod."

"If you have no objections, headmaster, I will stay with Macdonald till his uncle arrives. I have a spare, period four."

Taylor started to object, then obviously changed his mind.

With a ferocious scowl, he snarled at his secretary: "Inform me immediately Mr Lamont arrives," and slammed his office door behind him.

With a grim smile, Mr McLeod sat beside me. "I don't know what Mr Taylor intends. Did you explain to him the way you did to me? No, of course you didn't, you weren't in nearly long enough. Why not?"

"It would have done me more good to talk to his desk, sir. 'There are none so deaf as those who will not hear.' Isn't that the quote, sir?" I said. "There would have been no point at all." I shivered. "Uncle Alex is going to be mad."

"We can see the front gate from the window. Let's stand there and you tell me when your uncle appears."

We stood side by side at the window till I said: "That's him. The angry man coming up to the gate."

"Right, you sit down and wait."

It was almost five minutes later when Mr McLeod and Uncle Alex came into the outer office.

"Mrs Webster, would you please let Mr Taylor know Mr Lamont is here?"

Uncle Alex did look thoroughly annoyed, but to my surprise, he came right over.

"What on earth are we to do with you?" He took a pretend punch at my jaw and smiled.

"Ah, Mr Lamont, come in please," Mr Taylor said.

When Mr McLeod stepped forward with Uncle Alex, he added: "Only you, Mr Lamont."

"No, Mr Taylor," Uncle Alex said. "I'm not one of your pupils or your staff, thank God. Peter, come in please, and you too, Mr McLeod, if you would be so kind. Now, Mr Taylor, what is all this nonsense about? I have a store to run."

Mr Taylor was red, thin lipped, and his left temple twitched. "Your nephew was involved in an unprovoked assault on another student, Mr Lamont. I intend to suspend him, *sine die*. Until further notice that means."

"I know what it means, Mr Taylor, and your translation is not totally accurate, but that isn't relevant. I assume the other boy is also suspended? I see from your expression the answer is no. Why not? When will the hearing be with the Regional Education Committee? They have been notified, I trust? My solicitors will require a full set of the statements of all witnesses and participants."

Taylor was still flushed, but I thought he seemed more flustered than angry now. "I don't think we need be so formal, Mr Lamont. You may take my word, I very carefully investigated the whole incident before I came to my decision."

"Fine," Uncle Alex said. "Then I'll call the chairman of the Education Committee this afternoon. We should get this settled as soon as possible, and lawyers do tend to slow settlements down, don't they?"

"Well, I don't actually have written statements, Mr Lamont, and I have not yet consulted with the Committee," Taylor spluttered. "I can suspend, for cause, without consulting them you know."

"Yes, but not *sine die*, you can't," Uncle Alex put in.

"You haven't heard my story yet," I said. "And you haven't even spoken to Mr McLeod. He was right there."

"Be quiet, boy. Speak when you are spoken to," Taylor shouted.

"I will not stand by now and see my boy unfairly dealt with on the word of that short-sighted pipsqueak, Toady Johnston, and a boy who chooses to look like a warthog. I will take Peter with me now. To provide a cooling-off time. Joan Cameron's father is, incidentally, the new Inspector of Police for the Island, effective this morning. Thank you, Mr McLeod, for being here. Come, Peter."

Uncle Alex swept out of the office in great style, and ushered me quickly out of the school and down the street. Out of sight of the school building, he collapsed onto a bench at a bus stop.

"Wow. I'm shaking all over. I've never done that before. How did I do? Was I okay?"

"You were great, Uncle Alex, great. Thanks. I thought I was in for another whacking for sure."

Uncle Alex sagged. "I'm really sorry about that. Really I am. I was wrong, but I didn't have the guts to say so. I suppose I really didn't know how to talk to you about it. Let's take a walk. We can go and see if John Calder can join us for lunch. Fish and chips, okay? You can help at the store after till Taylor calls. We'll phone Aunt Jean to let her know, otherwise she'll worry when you're not home with Davey."

"What about the store, Uncle Alex?"

"Pat Morrison can handle it till I get back. This is more important."

We walked companionably down to the harbour, then out along the south shore, getting back to Uncle John's garage shortly before noon. Uncle John was surprised and pleased to see us, and readily agreed to join us. When I told him Aunt Ina had phoned Taylor, Uncle John scowled, then shrugged.

"I told her not to do it, but she doesn't listen. I'll see if I can do anything to stop this stupid interference. Maybe Father McIntyre can help."

"What about Taylor and this latest nonsense?" Uncle Alex said. "Mr McLeod, that teacher, seemed a very reasonable, fair minded man. You made a good impression on him, Peter."

"I don't think Taylor will be very keen to have a hearing with the Regional Education Committee," Uncle John said. "He's got friends on the council for sure, but Buchanan has more, and they're more powerful. I could drum up some support too, and we could turn it into a general look at discipline – amongst staff and students – since Taylor took over last year. I don't think he'll risk that. He thought Peter a friendless, family-less, complete outsider, and that we were simple, uneducated islanders. There's more than one kind of bully, Peter. I'll drop in on Buchanan on my way back to the garage and fill him in."

Back at Uncle Alex's store, I was put to work. First I dusted all the furniture in the show room, then started to uncrate and assemble occasional and coffee tables. I thoroughly enjoyed the experience and the newfound sense of comradeship with Uncle Alex.

The phone rang from time to time, but it was after three before Pat, Uncle Alex's assistant, shouted: "It's a Mr Taylor, Mr Lamont, he says it's important."

Uncle Alex motioned to me to pick up the extension phone, and held his forefinger to his lips.

"Lamont here. Can I help you?"

"Headmaster Taylor here, Mr Lamont. I have made my decision."

"In that case why call me, if there is nothing to discuss?"

"Mr Lamont, I will readmit Macdonald, and allow the suspension today to stand as the only punishment."

"Now hold hard there, Mr Taylor. I withdrew Peter today, to give us all some breathing space, to allow time for some mature reflection. If a suspension is to be logged on Peter's record, then I still want a full investigation of the whole affair, and a written report to me and the Committee chairman."

"Oh, very well, Mr Lamont. The suspension will not be logged. It will not appear anywhere on Macdonald's record."

"When you say nowhere, Mr Taylor, that includes your day book, your secretary's day book and Mr Johnston's day book?"

"Nowhere, Mr Lamont, in our school records."

"Fine, Mr Taylor."

"You can cut along, if you want to," Uncle Alex said. "I won't be ready to go home till closing time."

"Thanks again, Uncle Alex. I really thought you were great today."

 **Seventeen**

I arrived home before Davey, and had already told Aunt Jean and Grandpa the day's events before Davey arrived.

"Can I have something to eat, to tide me over till tea, Mum?" Davey shouted from the back door. "Have you seen Pete yet? Old Frosty Face looked like he'd sucked a lemon all afternoon."

"Peter's upstairs in your room, Davey," Aunt Jean called, and Davey clattered through the living room and up the stairs.

"How much bother are we in, Pete?" Davey said. "Did Dad whack you? Is he going to? Am I for it too?"

"It's all your fault, Davey. If you hadn't cheeked McLean, I wouldn't have got into a fight with him, and I wouldn't have been whacked by your dad. I'll kill you," I said, and advanced on Davey, grim faced.

Davey backed off, and fell back on the bed when its edge caught the back of his knees. I pounced with a whoop.

"I'll tickle you to death."

Davey shrieked and we wrestled till Aunt Jean shouted from the foot of the stairs: "For Heaven's sake you two, stop it before you bring the whole house down."

Laughing and breathless we stopped, and sat side by side on the floor.

"Aw, Pete, you gave me a fright. I thought you really meant it. That wasn't fair. What really happened? How mad is Dad?"

When I told Davey what had actually happened, Davey whooped and danced me round our room till Aunt Jean again shouted: "Davey, Peter. Stop it. What on earth has got into you? Wash up and get down here."

At tea in the evening, we were in high spirits, a shade too high for Uncle Alex and Aunt Jean apparently, since, right after tea, we were ordered out to run off some energy.

When we reached Mike's house, Mrs Buchanan met us at the door.

"Whoa, stop there, boys. Jean called to warn me you were on your way. Michael, the Apaches are here. You can go out, but I'll not have you three rioting in my house. You can come back for some cocoa later when you've run down a bit."

We roared off to the beach, and eventually, some energy run off, we slowed to talk of the day.

Davey and Mike's day had been successful and fairly uneventful. Mike had heard of my escapade, but in general it had created little interest outside my own class. We drifted towards the ice cream shop on the prom near the harbour, and bumped into Joan Cameron and a friend.

"This is Irene Wilkins, Pete. Irene, this is the boy I told you about."

I retold, yet again, the tale of my day.

"Wow, you should have seen it," Davey said. "It really wasn't a fight."

Davey danced round us, and described and demonstrated, while we walked back down to the prom and lounged in one of the shelters facing the sea.

"You're the boys that disappeared a year ago in the summer from the wood, aren't you?" Irene said. "Davey was in my class in elementary."

"Yes," I said, "but we don't remember anything. One minute we went into the wood, the next minute, McIntyre, the policeman, was there and it was a year later."

"There were five of you. What happened to the other two?" Irene asked.

"We don't know."

"It was really funny, Joan," Irene said. "Spooky. When they didn't turn up that night, Mrs Calder phoned the police. She really created because nobody really bothered till next day. They combed the whole island then, and showed their photos to all the ferry crews. Your folks came back from the States, Pete, when you didn't turn up.

"My dad says you were dressed funny when you came back. In dresses. And you had crossbows."

"Tunics, silly," Davey said. "We had shirts, tunics, hose, and boots."

"I'm not silly, Davey Lamont. Anyway I thought you couldn't remember."

"You are too, silly." Davey stuck his tongue out. "We were wearing them when McIntyre found us, weren't we? Pete's the one who was in a comma for three days."

"In a what?" Joan said.

"He means a coma." Irene laughed. "Anyway you must have looked cute, Davey Lamont. Dad says they were like long T-shirts, they covered your bum and no more."

Both girls giggled, and I felt my face flush.

"Pete, you're blushing. Look at him, Joan," Irene said.

"He goes red all over, everywhere, when he does that." Davey laughed and danced back out of my reach.

"How would you know?" Irene asked.

" 'Cause I've seen him, all of him, lots of times."

"If I get hold of you, Davey, I'll kill you," I said. My face felt as if it was on fire.

"He'll get you in bed tonight, Davey," Mike laughed.

"Do you two sleep together?" Irene asked.

"No, we don't," I snapped, almost in tears, and ran out of the shelter.

"Pete, they were only teasing." Joan touched my arm. "We've got to get back home. See you in school tomorrow. Come on, Irene. Dad'll fuss if I'm late."

When we moved off along the prom, Davey carefully kept out of my reach. "Are we going up to Mike's place? His mum said to come back for cocoa."

"Yes, okay, but we'll need to call home to say where we are; it's late."

We clattered in the back door, and Mrs Buchanan, who was on the phone, said: "They're here right now, Jean. I'll give them some cocoa and send them home. Fine. I'll call you tomorrow." She hung up. "Davey Lamont, keep your thieving hands off my biscuit tin. You can have toast, if you want, and one chocolate biscuit each, and that's it. You needn't 'Oh, Mrs Buchanan,' me with your fluttering eyelashes."

We sat round the kitchen table while Mrs Buchanan made cocoa and Davey was put to work making toast.

"I understand you had an interesting day, Peter," Mr Buchanan said.

"Pete's clicked already," Davey said. "Joan Cameron's ready to kill for him."

I rose towards Davey and bunched up my fists. "Sit down, Peter. Now!" At the sharp voice of command from Mr Buchanan, I slumped back into my chair. "Davey's teasing. Davey, Peter's had enough today, stow it."

"Sorry, Pete," Davey said, alarm, contrition, and concern mingled on his face. "I was only kidding, pulling your leg, honest. Okay?"

"Yeah, okay. I guess today has been pretty tough. I'm sorry."

On our walk home, Davey said: "Are we still friends?"

"Of course we are, but if Mr Buchanan hadn't stopped me, I'd have slugged you for sure. Cut out the wisecracks for a while."

"You've had toast and cocoa at the Buchanans, haven't you?" Aunt Jean said when we came in. "Then upstairs with you. Have a bath and go to bed."

We stripped quickly. Davey, undressed before me, said: "Me first," and raced for the bathroom. When I heard the water run in the bath, I closed the door and stood in front of the mirror to examine myself critically. My penis looked bigger, but it was difficult to be sure. It changed size depending on the temperature of the air round me, among other factors. There was a hint of hair, a very faint fuzz, beginning to appear. The door opened. Davey burst in.

"I forgot something … Wow. Joan should see you now."

I hit him, hard, and Davey fell. I followed him down and we wrestled. Davey was no match for my developing strength and current temper.

"Peter, stop that at once," Grandpa said. "Get up. Both of you. Now sit on your own beds."

Grandpa glared at both of us. He went to the door.

"It's all right, Jean. I'll deal with it. I'm here now anyway."

Davey was pale and shaking. "Are you all right, Grandpa? You don't look good. You're not supposed to hurry up the stairs."

"Yes, I'm fine, but no thanks to you two. What was that all about?"

Davey and I glowered at each other in silence.

The door was thrown open and Uncle Alex burst in. "Are you all right, Dad? I only stepped out for a minute. What in God's name were you two up to, to make Grandpa risk the stairs in a hurry like that? Put your shorts on both of you, and come down to my office. Bring the strop, Davey. Dad, do you need one of your pills?"

"No, Alex. It's all right, don't fuss. I've got one under my tongue. Give me your arm down to my room."

In silence, we pulled our shorts on, and didn't look at each other on our way down to Uncle Alex's office.

"Is Grandpa all right?" we said together, when Uncle Alex entered his office.

"I'm glad for your concern, belated though it is," Uncle Alex said. "Now, what was it all about? Your mum says it sounded like World War III starting. Now I see you in this light, Davey, you're going to have a black eye and a bruised jaw. What's the story or who's first?"

I swallowed. "It was my fault, Uncle Alex. Davey said something, and I lost my temper. Don't whack Davey."

"No, Dad. It was my fault. I teased Pete earlier and I knew he was uptight. I shouldn't have said what I did. I didn't think."

"What did you say? Exactly what was going on?"

We maintained a stony silence.

"Oh, I've had enough of this nonsense. It's much too late. Davey bend over ... Now you, Peter."

Uncle Alex gave us three strokes each.

Grandpa appeared at the door.

"Have you two any idea how silly you look there in your underwear, rubbing your bums?"

We rushed to Grandpa.

"Are you all right?" He put an arm round each of us. "Make up, boys? Life's too short for quarrels between good friends."

I put my hand out and Davey took it and we shook.

"Good night, Uncle Alex," I said.

"I'm still Uncle Alex, am I? I thought maybe I'd be promoted again."

I grinned. "No, Uncle Alex, we deserved that tonight, or at least I did."

"No, Dad, it was really my fault," Davey said.

"Well, let's not start the fight over again over whose fault it was," Uncle Alex said. "Go and make up with Mum. She really got a fright."

Davey and Grandpa left and I approached Uncle Alex.

"I'm really sorry about tonight, Uncle. Especially after how great you were today. I really appreciated you standing up for me the way you did. Thanks."

"You awake, Pete?" Davey whispered from his bed later.

"Yes, Davey."

"I'm sorry I bugged you today. Friends, Pete?"

"Yes, Davey, friends. Mr Buchanan will say I over-reacted, I bet. It wasn't all your fault. I was too quick to fly off the handle, but oh boy, you sure did make me mad. Sorry about the eye."

"That's okay. It'll look great in the morning."

 **Eighteen**

We were still sound asleep, next morning, when Aunt Jean came into our room.

"Come on you two, up. I've shouted till I'm hoarse. Feet on the floor."

"You go first, Pete," Davey mumbled and rolled over.

"No, Davey," Aunt Jean said, and slapped his rump. "Up. I want to talk to Pete for a minute. Move your carcass, Davey Lamont."

"Ow, Mum, careful. I'm still sore from last night. Okay. Okay. I'm moving."

I sat up in bed and Aunt Jean sat on the edge of my bed.

"Are you happy here, with us?"

"Yes, Aunt Jean, why?"

"Well, there was the fight last night."

"I'm sorry, that won't happen again, I promise."

"No, I'm not blaming you. Although you're not really all that much older than Davey, he's the baby of the family and a bit spoilt, in some ways you seem much older than Davey. I wondered if this will make for difficulties between you. If it is a problem, the Buchanans will be very pleased to have you stay there."

"Do you want me to go, Aunt Jean?"

"No, Peter. Heavens no. I want you and Davey to be happy, that's all. Uncle Alex has taken to you much better than I could ever have expected. I was amazed, and very pleased, at how he handled the business at the school yesterday. The pair of you were as thick as thieves over that. It really was a pity about last night."

"Last night won't spoil anything. Last night, Uncle Alex was right. Davey and I deserved it. Davey and I are all right, even brothers fall out at times, but we are friends, and more like brothers now than cousins."

Aunt Jean smiled and leaned forward to kiss me. "Hustle, the pair of you. We're all late this morning."

At the breakfast table, Uncle Alex seemed relaxed. He smiled at us and commented jocularly on Davey's black eye. He got up to go, then produced the strop, and placed it on the table. Davey edged back, but Uncle Alex said: "You're both past this now. Your behaviour, afterwards, last night was quite grown up. Jean, you can throw this out. I won't use it again."

Davey grinned.

"That doesn't mean you'll get away with anything, Davey. I expect you to be a bit more grown up, that's all."

When we picked Mike up, he whistled. "Wow, Davey. Where did you get that keeker? – that's a black eye to you, Pete. I haven't seen as good a one in years."

Davey grinned and I felt my face flush.

"We were horsing around, and my face got in the way of Pete's fist," Davey said. "It was an accident."

"I'll believe you, thousands wouldn't." Mike laughed. "If I had been Pete, I'd have punched your lights out last night. You really were pushing it."

"Come on, Mike," Davey said. "Pete's had enough, back us up. It really was my fault. Even Dad said so after he whacked us."

"Davey, with a friend like you, who needs enemies," Mike said. "Just joking, Pete, just joking. I don't need a matching keeker. Come on brothers, let's go."

Irene pounced on us as we came through the school gates. "Dad says you three are definitely weird. He sent samples of the material from your dresses–"

"Tunics, silly," Davey interrupted.

"Well, whatever. Anyway, Dad sent the samples somewhere for testing, dating. He says they test out at some point in the twelfth century, but he's never seen such rapid deterioration of a sample. They went from being used, but in good condition, to dust in weeks. What happened to your eye, Davey? Who gave you it?"

"Nobody gave it to me, I had to work for it."

Mike grinned. "Now isn't that the truth."

"Have you three fallen out?" Irene said.

Mike laughed. "No, Davey had an accident, that's all. There's the bell. We'd better get to form."

Some of my classmates looked at me a little curiously, but there were no comments. We did have McLeod for English, I was glad to see, but I was less pleased to learn Johnston taught French and Latin to my class.

Nineteen

"Ah, Macdonald, you've decided to join us. The holiday not long enough for you? Felt the need of an extra day, did we?"

The mathematics teacher's smile took the sting out of his words, as he handed me the texts the others had been given the day before. I'd always been a good student, so I'd had no problems in the morning classes, and the maths certainly seemed reasonable.

The last double period of the day was a games period. For physical education, the boys from both academic secondary classes were time-tabled together, so when we entered the changing room we found Spiky McLean and Harry both there. Harry swallowed hard and backed into a corner when I walked up to him.

"I noticed you didn't join in yesterday, Harry. That was a good move. I don't expect you to join with us, but if you keep out we'll get on fine."

"Ah don't want any bother," Harry said.

Other boys drifted in while we spoke.

"Go on McLean, have a go at him," a voice said. "That was a fluke, yesterday."

I turned and met the eye of the speaker, who reddened, and turned away.

"If you think so, you have a go," McLean said, "but deal me out."

"What's the hold up here?" An adult voice shouted into the locker room. "Get changed you lot, then outside."

The boys all scrambled to strip and change into their sports clothes.

"Wow, see their backs? Look at the scars. What happened to you?"

The other youngsters crowded round us. I sensed no danger or antagonism, only curiosity, and I didn't resist when the others touched my back and Davey's.

"Out, you lot," the physical education teacher shouted, and the group broke for the door.

Davey and I were in good condition and had no problem at all with the conditioning training the teacher had in store for us. By the end of the double period, most of the boys were winded, but Davey and I were still fresh.

"You two are in remarkably good shape," the teacher said. "Have you been working out under supervision?" But he didn't wait for a reply before hustling everyone into the change room.

"Showers, everyone," the teacher shouted. The boys groaned and grumbled.

"God, I'm knackered," someone said.

"We should kill that sadistic bastard," a second said.

"I would, but I don't have the strength left," groaned another.

"Look at Macdonald and Lamont: fresh as bleeding daisies."

Some boys crowded round Davey, and I tensed for battle, but it seemed harmless banter. Annoying to Davey, no doubt, but harmless.

"How did you get that black eye, Lamont?"

"I bet Irene Wilkins gave him it. He fancies her, don't you Lamont?"

"No, it would be Joan Cameron."

"I'll bet it was Joan. She probably found him trying to make out with Irene, and she clocked him one. Like she did Forsythe yesterday."

"Maybe he was trying to make out with Joan Cameron and Peter Macdonald clocked him."

Davey's shorts were snatched out of his hands, and he was spun naked. Everyone laughed.

"Leave him be," I said, "that's enough. Get dressed, Davey."

"Listen to big brother, Davey dear," said the boy who held Davey's shorts. At my glare, and purposeful advance, he threw Davey his shorts and held up both hands, palms toward me.

"A joke, Macdonald. A joke."

Twenty

We met up with Mike when we left school and chattered about the day. On the whole, school was going well for all three of us, but we agreed the routine was very tough after the freedom of the previous year. By the time we reached the Lamont's house, Davey was quieter than usual, quiet and thoughtful. So much so, Aunt Jean asked if he was all right or if there had been some sort of trouble.

"No, Mum. We went up to the grove and got to thinking about last year," Davey said. Mike dug him in the ribs and he yelped.

"Have you all remembered what happened last year, then?" Aunt Jean said.

"No, Mum," Davey hastened to answer. "It made us feel sad, sort of, that's all. Can Mike stay to tea?"

"Yes, if he wants to. There's plenty, but he'd better phone home first, and let his mum know."

After tea we dropped Mike's school bag off at his home, then made for the prom. Joan and Irene met up with us when we approached the shelter in which we had talked the night before.

"What do they want?" Davey said. "I wanted to talk. Just us, without any outsiders. Especially not girls."

"It's okay, we can talk later," I said, and greeted the girls.

We collected at the shelter, but on this mild evening we lounged on the benches beside the shelter looking out to sea.

"What did happen to you last year?" Joan said. "Dad had the file home last night and he and Mum talked about it after dinner. They only fenced the wood ten years ago. The day you lot came back, they'd had the gamies – all the gamekeepers from the Duke's estate – and police patrol the outside of the fence and the gates were padlocked. The Duke paid for the extra police time. McIntyre was checking the patrols when he heard you and ran into the wood. He had an ambulance take the three of you to the hospital and it was Irene's dad he sent for to see you. It sounds like they really thought Pete might die."

Irene interrupted. "I heard Dad talk to Mum about it, too. He said the boys had obviously been living rough, but were in very good shape. They had scratches, old and new, on their arms and legs, and all three had been whipped or flogged hard enough to break or tear the skin. Peter didn't seem to have any obvious injuries, but was in deep shock." Irene giggled. "There were photographs of all three of you in the file. Front, back, and side, in the buff. You really looked cute, Davey."

Davey chased her, and Irene ran, giggling, down the sea front. She doubled back, and she and Davey danced round Joan, while Irene kept Joan between her and Davey.

"Help me. She saw your photos too."

Mike and I, both red faced, laughed self consciously but made no move.

"It's all right, Davey. I didn't really see your photograph," Irene gasped, out of breath. "They're in the file all right, but Dad doesn't leave them lying around. Anyway, I'd get killed if Dad caught me at any of his files."

Davey stopped his pursuit of Irene.

"Dad said Waddell, the shrink, couldn't shake your stories, but he was sure you'd been together and you were like a combat unit, a potentially nasty trio."

"Does your dad know you're seeing us, Joan?" I said.

"We are not seeing you. Not the way you mean anyway. We are in class together. Irene and I happened to bump into you tonight."

"And last night," Davey said.

"We've got to go now. I said I wouldn't be out late," Joan said.

We walked back towards town with the girls and chatted generally about school, the other kids and the teachers. When the girls reached the turn off to their home area, Irene laughed.

"Oh, I forgot. Dad said two of the boys were pubescent and one was pre-pubescent. I must see if I can get a peak at those photos. I bet you do look cute, Davey."

"Oh, Irene, that's not fair. See him blush. Does he blush all over too, Pete, like he says you do? Come on Irene, run."

 **Twenty One**

At Mike's house we saw a black Rolls Royce, shiny and spotless, in the roadway at the foot of the drive. A uniformed chauffeur glanced curiously at us as we came up the driveway, after we walked all round the car.

"That's not an army car," Mike said. "I wonder what bigwig is visiting Dad."

We went in the back door.

Mrs Buchanan called through from the living room: "That you, Michael? Have Davey and Peter gone home?"

"Yes, Mum, it's me. Pete and Davey are here with me. Can we have some cocoa?"

"Come in here, please."

"Uh, oh," Davey said, "that sounds like trouble. Have we done anything recently?"

We trooped through to the living room. A tall middle-aged man stood beside Mr Buchanan at the window. He turned and focused his gaze on me. I stared back and we looked at each other until the stranger shifted his attention to Davey.

"Your Grace, may I present my son Michael, and his friends Davey Lamont, and Peter Macdonald.

"Boys, this is the current Duke."

Mike and Davey bowed as I had taught them, it now seemed so long ago, and murmured: "Your Grace."

Fractionally after Mike and Davey, I gave my half bow, half nod. "My Lord Duke, you are a direct linear descendant of the first duke, are you not? We are pleased to meet you."

"Yes, Peter, I am. I represent the direct male line from the first duke, William Gerald, in the twelfth century. He was killed in a hunting accident while his son was still an infant. My hobby is the family history. I have researched it very thoroughly. There are some very nasty stories about the first duke. He seems to have been, in some respects, a thoroughly unpleasant individual. There are also some very curious folk tales or legends about his time, and the time of his son, the second duke, handed down within the family.

"Most of them centre around some very shadowy characters, variously referred to as: the Warlocks, who are Boys; the Boys, who are Warlocks; the Lords of Möbius; the Brothers of Keith the Cripple; the Companions of Davey, Master of the Demon Skin. It is not at all clear in the legends if these all refer to the same group of men or to different groups."

Mrs Buchanan bustled in with a tray of china and a tea pot. "Davey, go and bring in the other tray, and don't eat any of the biscuits on the way."

Davey grinned.

Seated, the Duke went on. "As I was saying, there are interesting stories of the time. There are several about an apparently very influential individual, who was guardian to the second Duke while he was infant, and right-hand man and advisor to him when he grew to be an adult.

"There are two different names attached to this individual: one is Andrew and the other is Peter. From other evidence in the stories, it's unlikely these were the same man, but it's difficult to say. There is probably some confusion over who did what also. In some stories, Peter is the illegitimate son of the first Duke. In others, he is the ghost of the first Duke, purified by his death at the

Hunt. This ghost aspect of the stories is carried on in the stories in which Peter is really the good side of the Duke, somehow separated, sent back to kill the Duke at the Hunt. Peter seems to have killed the Duke and vanished, to reappear a year later. Others say, having killed the Duke, Peter, wisely, went to earth for a year. The stories all agree that matters were not going well for the dowager duchess or the infant duke till Peter did reappear."

"Ask him of Roland de Guisse, Peter."

"Your Grace," I said, "why are you telling us all this? Why did you come here?"

The Duke laughed. "The Major said you would not easily be startled into betraying yourself. I think I can guess your story, the real story, of your past year."

"What do you know of Roland de Guisse, Your Grace?" I said.

The Duke drew back slightly and raised his eyebrows, then grinned.

"No, My Lord Peter of Möbius, you first. What do you know of him?"

I sat, head slightly to one side for a little, while I listened to my Duke, Gerald, in my head. Mr Buchanan started to speak, but the Duke cut him off with a sharp chopping movement of his right hand.

I laughed. "That must be a family gesture of command, Your Grace. Inherited no doubt. We last saw it used by Duke William Gerald. Roland de Guisse was an emissary from the royal court, a spy. He appeared from time to time, always with some trouble in his wake."

I paused. I could feel my face change as Gerald took over.

"He feigned friendship, and I, of course, affected belief in his professions. I was not blameless, but he encouraged me in my excesses and oft provided the means for them. Master Simmons was his man, bought and paid for. What of him after my departure at the final hunt?"

"My God. Who's speaking?"

The Duke was pale and I could scarcely hear him.

"Answer my question, man," my Duke went on. "Answer William, Duke of This Island and the Lands Beyond."

"Roland de Guisse is mentioned in the stories: someone who attempted to usurp the second duke in his infancy, but he was held at bay by Andrew and Peter, or by Andrew, or by Peter. He seems to have died in some battle at about the time of the second duke's majority."

"Good."

I felt my face go slack, and my voice returned to its youthful quality. I blinked and shook my head.

"Your Grace, Duke William Gerald wanted to speak to you direct. I hope we did not startle you too much."

The Duke laughed. "Startle me, Lord Peter? Mrs Buchanan almost lost two pieces of her good china and it is the closest I have come to wetting myself since I served under the Major. Startle is hardly strong enough."

Everyone laughed, but the Duke went on. "I would like you boys to believe I am your friend. Major, anything that is required for the boys, I will provide. Privacy, I cannot absolutely guarantee, but if it is within my power, I will provide it. The boys must visit me and see the history of the time of Duke William Gerald in my family records. Some legend, some fact and little to show which is which. I must go now, you have given me much to think of. I had intended to be off-island again most of this year, but my other estates can fend for themselves. I should be here."

We all stood when the Duke did. The Duke put a hand on Davey's shoulder.

"You must be Davey, Master of the Demon Skin. You haven't said very much today, but I imagine conversation with a mouth full of biscuit is difficult even for you. Perhaps, Mrs Buchanan, we should think of either a biscuit allowance or a biscuit safe? This has been a most interesting visit. Thank you Mrs Buchanan, Major. I hope to see you again boys, soon. Goodbye."

To a chorus of, "goodbye, Your Grace," the Duke left, and Mr Buchanan walked him to his car.

 **Twenty Two**

When Mr Buchanan returned he looked very thoughtful.

"Helen, would you make some cocoa for the boys, if they want it?"

There was a chorus of, "yes, please," and Davey added hopefully, "toast, too?"

Mrs Buchanan gripped Davey by the neck and marched him off to the kitchen.

"Come, Master Davey of the Hollow Legs, work for your supper."

Mr Buchanan turned to Mike and me. "The Duke had guessed your story, boys. I didn't tell him. He is a very intelligent man and is apparently steeped in his family history. I think he is sincere in his wish to know and help you, but his motives are less clear.

"Peter, he supports your decision to remain on the island for school, and he will provide the services of his solicitors, free, for any legal work needed. He also would prefer that you stay with the Lamonts. You are related to the Duke at several points in your family tree and his."

"How is Mum's family related to the present Duke?"

"Apparently through the one you called Andrew of the Forest. Andrew and the first Duke were second cousins. Andrew had two daughters. In some of the stories, one of them married the Peter of the legend, but in all, your mother's family descends from one of these daughters. The two families intermarried, off and on, until the Covenanting Wars, when the Duke's family remained Catholic and your mother's family sided with the Covenanters."

Mr Buchanan stopped and looked at me for what seemed a long time. "You know, Peter, you do resemble the Duke as a young man."

"Not again, please."

At that, Mrs Buchanan and Davey arrived with the cocoa and toast.

"Now lads, back to more immediate and practical matters," Mr Buchanan said. "The Maths and French tutor for all of you will be here tomorrow evening at seven. I expect you to work hard for him."

He looked at the three of us.

"We really need a small gym. You all need to get back into training or you'll get flabby. Look at you, Davey."

Mr Buchanan grasped a fold of skin on Davey's side and Davey, ticklish, squirmed and laughed.

"Careful, you two. You'll have the coffee table over. Stop it Murdoch, you're worse than the boys," Mrs Buchanan said.

"Joking apart, boys," Mr Buchanan said, "you were in first-rate condition when you arrived back, and unless you keep up training you'll lose that. I wouldn't want you over-trained, but you should keep your edge."

"Major, why did the Duke come to you?" I said. "I don't mean to be disrespectful, but if he is interested in us, Davey and myself, as family, it's really nothing to do with you. He should have contacted the Lamonts."

I sat, face flushed. Mrs Buchanan opened her mouth to speak, but changed her mind. Davey and Mike looked at me, glanced quickly at Mr Buchanan, and looked away.

Mike's face, plain to read, said: 'Run for cover, storm coming.'

Mr Buchanan cleared his throat.

"The Duke called on me because he once served under my command. He was a young lieutenant and I, a captain. That, and the fact that Michael, my son, was one of the group. Your arrival here this evening was chance. It simply happened to work out. So there is no case to answer there.

"I did, however, discuss your affairs with the Duke, at his instigation, but without your knowledge or consent. For that I do apologise. It was presumptuous of me."

Mike looked puzzled. This was obviously not the reaction he had expected. Mrs Buchanan looked relieved. I excused myself and left the living room.

In the hallway, I turned when Mr Buchanan followed me.

"I'm sorry, Mr Buchanan. That came out as rude and ungrateful. I didn't mean it to be. I jumped the gun, didn't I? I'm sorry. I guess I was annoyed at the Duke stepping in and thinking," I paused and laughed, "giving me the impression he thought he could take over and run us."

Mr Buchanan took my arm and led me through to the kitchen.

"Sit down, Peter. I am not offended or hurt. You simply reached a new stage, before I expected it, and, in some ways, before you were prepared for it. All right?"

I wasn't quite sure what he meant.

"You and Grandpa Lamont are the best thing that's happened to me in a long time, thanks."

"Let's go back in."

Twenty Three

Work with the tutors went well. Despite our year away from school we had no particular difficulties with academic work, though Davey had to be hounded to study most of the time.

Physical education and organised games had never been favourite classes for me before our year in the forest, but we were all fit and active and found endurance type activities easier than our classmates did. I even found myself enjoying them. Davey and Mike were both soccer players and made the teams for their age groups. I joined track and field. We were all in the Judo classes run by Alf Turner, the school janitor; the man who had picked us up the night the Campbells chased us at the quarries.

The feud with Aunt Ina continued. I visited Uncle John and Aunt Ina once a week, and often dropped in to see Uncle John at his garage. Letters from both Mom and Dad arrived regularly. I began to dread Dad's blasts about my disobedience in staying with the Lamonts and in not obeying Aunt Ina.

In mid-November, Aunt Ina was all smiles when I came to brunch. "Your father is going to court to claim custody. I know, John," she hurried on when Uncle John tried to interrupt. "Such an order would have no legal standing here for us, but I'm sure it would be taken into account by any court here in deciding who should have custody of Peter."

I stormed out, too angry to observe the usual social niceties. Not wishing to go home till I cooled down and unwilling to dump more of my problems on the Buchanans, I went down to the harbour. When the afternoon ferry came in, the first car off was a black, chauffeur-driven Rolls Royce. It stopped abruptly, much to the annoyance of the crewman directing traffic, and the Duke jumped out. He waved his chauffeur on, and crossed to where I stood.

"Peter, my boy. How are you?"

"Good afternoon, Your Grace."

"Let's stroll a little. I've wanted to talk to you for some time. The Major says you are all doing well and I'm not to interfere without your knowledge and consent."

I laughed, remembering my temper with Mr Buchanan.

"This is awkward, Peter. You are both the first Duke William Gerald, my ancestor, and a boy who is most certainly a relative. In appearance you could well be my son."

I groaned, then laughed. "I've been through this before, My Lord."

"Yes, I know. If one legend and family records are correct, you are also probably directly related in your own right. Peter of Möbius, husband to Margaret, eldest daughter of Andrew of the Forest."

I felt my face flush.

"There we are, Peter. Let us go home, please. You dream of Margaret. You know you do."

"Why are you blushing?" the Duke said. "Well, no matter, none of my business. As I was saying, our relationships being so tangled, I feel awkward having you address me so formally."

"What should I call you, sir?"

"My intimates call me Gerry. Gerald is my Christian name, but that is a shade too familiar."

"Uncle Gerry?"

The Duke laughed.

"That will certainly set tongues wagging, but why not? It will certainly explain the family resemblance. We are almost at the tearoom on the point. Let's have afternoon tea. I don't think I've been in there since I was about your age."

Over the tea and cakes, on impulse, I told the Duke of Aunt Ina's news today. After questioning me closely on how I felt about it, the Duke noted down the addresses of both parents. "I can clear this up, but only if you wish me to. I do not wish to seem to be interfering."

"Please, do what you can."

We parted on that and I felt much happier on my way home.

Next morning, the headmaster sent for me.

"Your Aunt, Mrs Calder I mean, has phoned to say she is now your legal guardian. I am not prepared to get into any legal battles over you or your custody, boy. I shall follow her wishes and have your documents prepared for forwarding to St Martin's."

"Might I make a phone call, sir?"

"Well, this is most irregular, but yes, I suppose so. Only a local call mind, boy."

Taylor motioned me to use the phone on his desk, but made no move to leave the office.

I searched my pocket for the scrap of paper with the Duke's number on it, then dialled.

The male voice at the other end seemed amused when I asked for Uncle Gerry, but put me through. I quickly explained.

"Come, boy, I haven't all day to waste on this nonsense," Taylor grumbled.

"Can you take the phone please, sir?"

"Well! Headmaster Taylor here," he snapped into the phone, then held the receiver away as if it had bitten him, and glared at me. The phone squawked. He put it back cautiously to his ear and listened.

"I had no idea, Your Grace.

"Certainly, Your Grace.

"I understand perfectly, My Lord. Your solicitors will so advise the Education Committee? I will certainly make no move without further instruction. No. No, Mrs Calder has not produced any papers or documents. Good morning, My Lord."

Taylor put down the phone, glared at me, then his face contorted.

Is that supposed to be a smile?

"I was not aware His Grace was a friend of yours."

"He isn't particularly, sir. We're related. May I go now?"

"Yes, Macdonald, of course. I'm glad you're to stay with us. I would have thought His Lordship would have wanted you at St Martin's. His is one of the few Catholic families to retain their holdings more or less intact through the ages. By all reports you are an excellent student."

Later in the week, as I stepped in the door after school, I answered the phone.

"Peter, Mom here. I hoped I'd catch you. It's shortly after eleven in the morning here. Listen. This has been rather an incredible week. Your dad phoned to say he would be taking legal action for custody. On Monday, a lawyer came to see me, right out of the blue. He said he'd been retained by an interested party to represent me – you, I suppose, really. Anyway, he was a real high-powered, high-priced too I expect, character. He left me quite breathless. Tuesday afternoon your dad's lawyer called to say your dad was dropping his action for custody, without prejudice, whatever that means. To cap it all, your dad phoned today, all peeved. His Bishop, no less, had contacted him through his lawyer with the message, 'Leave the boy alone'. Talk about *ex cathedra*.

Your dad couldn't have been more surprised. So, you stay with Jean and Alex, and attend the local school. All right?"

At last, able to get a word in, I chattered to Mom about what I'd been doing since I last wrote. I didn't tell about the Duke's involvement. So far, I'd told no one except Charlie and Mr Buchanan.

 # Twenty Four

School and home routine set, time sped past. The tutors hired by Mr Buchanan decided we had caught up enough in Mathematics and French, and stopped seeing us.

Irene and Joan were now established members of the group, although Davey still grumbled from time to time about their inclusion.

There was no real pairing off. The girls appeared and went home together, and so did we.

When my church held a dance for the youth group, I invited Joan to go with me. Joan was delighted to be asked, but was a shade nervous of going unless Irene was also invited.

At brunch at Aunt Ina's, I mentioned my dilemma.

"Get two more tickets, Pete," Uncle John said, "and ask Mike and Irene to go with you. I'll pay for their tickets if you're a bit short of cash. Mike's been a real help to me since he started coming down to the garage. He says I'm the next best thing to a blacksmith."

"That would be great, thanks," I said.

"What are you two cooking up?" Aunt Ina said when she brought through the meal.

I explained.

"Oh, that won't be necessary," she said. "I've already invited Cathie Small to go with you."

"You've what?" Uncle John and I said together.

"Cathie Small is a nice girl, you'll like her, Peter. She's the daughter of one of my Guild ladies."

"I've already asked Joan."

"You said she hasn't accepted yet, and I've already told Cathie and her mother."

"Then you take her," I said.

"There is no need to be rude or to shout, Peter. Cathie is a nice Catholic girl and is a much more appropriate partner than that Joan Cameron."

"I asked Charlie – Father McIntyre – if it was all right to ask Joan. He said, yes. In fact, he said we should put the tickets on sale in the school."

Aunt Ina snorted. "I've spoken to Father McGuire, but he has made no attempt to curb Father McIntyre. I shall write to the Bishop. I don't approve of these mixed dances."

"Come on, Ina," Uncle John said. "They've always been like that here. Peter's dad met his mother at such a social."

"And look what that led to."

"Me, for one thing, Aunt Ina."

Uncle John laughed, but Aunt Ina scowled.

"That's a most improper comment, Peter. I don't know what has got into you. My dear brother – your father – should certainly have gone into the church."

"Well, I, for one, am glad he didn't, otherwise we wouldn't have Peter," Uncle John said. "Let's not quarrel again."

Aunt Ina maintained a stony silence while Uncle John and I chatted during the meal.

Next day, I waited by the gate at school till Cathie came in.

"Cathie, I don't know how to say this," I said, "but I suppose straight out is best. I'm asking Joan Cameron to the dance. My Aunt had no right to ask you without talking to me first."

To my relief, Cathie laughed.

"Mum and I had a row last night about it. She said I couldn't offend the Dragon Lady – sorry Peter, Mrs Calder, but Harry has asked me."

"Great. So you're going with Harry?"

"Why is Harry so scared of you? When I told him about your aunt's invitation he backed right off. 'Ah'm no' messin' wi' them,' he said."

"It's nothing, Cathie. Harry's got a good imagination. Tell him it's okay. We'll all be at the dance."

The night of the dance, Davey was not speaking to anyone. He didn't really want to go, I was sure, but he seemed furious Mike and I would go without him.

We met the girls on the sea front as usual. Our entry at the dance attracted no particular attention. I had been afraid some of the other parishioners might be bigoted like Aunt Ina and equally against Mike and the girls being with me. The older teenagers, the majority, simply ignored us, busy with their own concerns. Some of my classmates and Mike's were there and made comments, but they were in the main good natured banter and we replied in kind. Tommy, whom I had not seen since our encounter on the beach, was there with Harry and Cathie. He said hello, but kept his distance.

At one point in the evening I found myself close to both Harry and Tommy and asked them if they had heard anything of the Campbells.

Harry and Tommy looked at each other, then Tommy said: "Donald and Murray are with some mates on the mainland till their trial comes up. The Old Man has jumped bail. No one knows where he is. So Ted's in care."

"What about his mother?" I said.

"She's been dead for at least a couple of years."

Harry shrugged.

"The Old Man used to beat up on her, so Ted said anyway. Ted said he'd kill the Old Man when he was big enough."

Joan tugged at my sleeve.

"Come on, Pete. It's supposed to be a dance."

When we left the hall, we drifted back down to the sea front, still a group, but now with a loose pairing, Joan with me, and Irene with Mike. We leaned against the railing and watched the tide come in. Greatly daring, I took Joan's hand. She did not immediately snatch it back. Encouraged, I squeezed. I was working up the nerve to kiss Joan when Irene's voice said, out of the dark: "We'd best get home, Joan. It's late."

Still hand in hand, we walked to Irene's house where the front door immediately opened and two male figures appeared.

"It's Dad," both Irene and Joan said.

" 'Night, Irene," Mike and I chorused.

Joan's father joined us at the gate.

"Good evening, boys."

"Good evening, sir."

"Had a good time, Joan?"

"Oh, yes, Dad. It was fun."

"Well, say good night. Mum's waiting up."

"Oh, Dad."

"Say good night, and run along. I want to talk to the boys for a minute."

"That was fun, Pete. Thanks."

The three of us stood and watched her run three houses up the street, then turn and wave at us from the open door. We waved back.

"I'll walk part way with you, boys," Inspector Cameron said.

We walked in silence for a short time.

Inspector Cameron studied both of us in the light of the street lamp. I thought he seemed flushed, but it was difficult to say.

"Nothing personal, boys, but Wilkins and I are not too happy about Joan and Irene spending so much time with you. You're too old for the girls."

"Oh, Mr Cameron, we're about the same age as the girls. Pete certainly is and I'm only a year older. We haven't done anything wrong, any of us. Please."

Inspector Cameron sighed. "Joan likes you, Pete. With her anyway I'm sure you're only a boy. However, I can't help feeling I'm safer under your escort than you are under mine." He paused. "You boys were in the vicinity the night the Campbells had their accident, weren't you?"

"Yes, sir," I said and went on to tell him the official story of our being disturbed by noises and frightened at our camp out, and going back down the firebreak road, where we were lucky enough to get a ride into town.

"Uh huh. You were frightened by some noise in the dark wood were you? I see."

Again we walked in silence for a short time.

"Usually, when kids are scared, they run. The whole area was searched because Donald Campbell kept babbling on about 'some kids who were not kids', who had trapped him and his brother. There was no trace of a camp out. No signs of panic flight. No tracks that couldn't have been made by small animals, except the blundering trail left by the Campbells from a small clearing to the cliff edge. Ted wouldn't – or couldn't – say anything except that his brothers had run off after something and had not come back. Donald was terrified when he was found. Glad even to see the police."

"Sir, why weren't we questioned if you suspected us?"

"Because there was no evidence to put you at the scene. The Campbells did not mention you by name. It was clearly an accident. The Campbells, Murray and Donald anyway, had been drinking.

"It was you lot that set up Neil Campbell, wasn't it?"

"Set up is hardly fair, sir," I said. "Is there any question the Campbells were fencing stolen property?"

"No, Peter. No question. A lot of the stuff at the Logan place came from truck hijacks and warehouse break-ins, but nothing to connect the Campbells to it till the night Murray was found there. How did you fix it?"

"No big deal, sir," I said. "We arranged for Davey to bump into Ted and to pretend to run away. Of course, Ted caught him. Davey squealed he knew where I had put the keys I took from Murray."

"What keys? When did you take them from Murray?"

"That's a long story, sir. Davey told Ted that I hid the keys at the Logan place, but he could find them if Ted would leave him be after."

"But it was Murray that was found there—"

"Yes, sir. Ted told Murray that he could get his keys and Murray wanted to get back at me. So he had Ted tell Davey that I had to be there."

"As you knew he would, no doubt." Inspector Cameron scowled. "Go on."

"There isn't much else. When Murray turned up, Mike dropped a net over him and we roped him. In the gardener's hut, Mike sat on him and held his nose while I poured whisky into him. When he was drunk enough, we took the rope and net away, set a small fire at the far end of the hut, in the cigarettes, and called the fire brigade and the police."

"And Ted?"

"He was busy chasing Davey. He got a bit of a fright when he caught him. We're not the softies we were a year ago."

The Inspector frowned. "And you wonder why Wilkins and I are worried? Everything in the hut and cellar had Campbell fingerprints on it. We were able to arrest Old Man Campbell, Murray and Donald. Since his mother was dead, Ted was taken into care. Old Man Campbell almost killed Murray in the exercise yard. I don't imagine any of them are feeling too friendly towards you. I'll leave you here, boys."

He turned away, took two steps then stopped and turned again.

"I've heard word, never mind how, that Neil Campbell has been seen on the mainland, after he jumped bail. Word has it he talked about killing you, or having you killed. I can't take any official action, not even to put men on to watch you without some good reason for the log. After all, there is no connection between you and the Campbells, is there? I think the odds are stacked against Campbell. I don't want him dropping dead unexpectedly in my manor."

"He won't, sir," I said.

As the Inspector turned to go, a figure stepped out of the shadows.

"Good evening, Inspector, boys."

"Hi, Mr Turner," Mike and I said.

"You're Turner from the school?" the Inspector said.

"Yes, sir. Mind if I walk with you a bit, boys? Good night, Inspector."

"Were you following us, Mr Turner?" I said.

"Yes and no."

"Does Dad know Neil Campbell's back in the area?" Mike said. "Did you hear what Mr Cameron said?"

Turner nodded.

"Here you are, Mike. See you at school."

Turner and I walked without talking the remainder of the way to the Lamont's. At the gate, Turner stopped.

"For the next day or so there'll always be someone around, sir. You might or might not see them." He grinned. "Just don't kill anyone that doesn't go for you first, okay, sir?"

Tears in my eyes, I grabbed at Turner's arm.

"Why? Mr Turner, why? And why the sir?"

Turner smiled.

"The Major's got our whole unit standing to: Father Charlie's back in business; McLeod was looking out for you even before the call went out; the Duke isn't going off-island for the first winter I know of. I don't know who or what you are, but things sure pop around you, sir."

"I prefer Pete, Mr Turner."

I ran into the house.

Aunt Jean was still up when I got home, but I called good night to her and ran past, up to our room.

Davey snored gently and I stripped quickly and slipped into bed, or tried to. No matter what I did I couldn't get my feet more than a third of the way down the bed.

While I struggled to remake my bed in the dark, and cursed to myself, I heard Davey giggle.

 **Twenty Five**

On Monday evening when Davey and I called for Mike, Mr Buchanan called me in.

"You boys go on," he said. "Peter will catch up on you. He and I have to talk."

Mr Buchanan looked at me in silence and for a moment, I wondered if I'd done something wrong.

"You remember I said we needed something like a gym?"

"Yes, some time ago."

I waited.

"I spoke to the Duke about it. I thought he might find us some space on the estate."

"And?"

"Peter, he's not interfering, or at least he doesn't mean to. You know the empty double shop right next door to mine?"

I nodded.

"Well he's had it gutted and fitted out as a small gym, complete with weight-lifting stuff. The flats above were empty, so he had a steel spiral stair put in. You can go from the gym to upstairs, to wash or change, without going outside. He's had a doorway knocked through from the cupboard in my darkroom."

"When did he do all this?"

"In the last three weeks. Money talks. It was all off-island men and everything came in sealed packing cases. No one knows but them and us."

"But you've known for three weeks?"

"No, Peter, only since Thursday last when they put through the doorway. I knew something was being done next door, but not what or why. I've been considering when and how to tell you since then."

"Can I see it before we tell the others?"

"Yes, The Group will be there at eight. Come with me. You can meet up with Davey and Michael here later."

Mr Buchanan walked with me to his shop and let me into the store next door and left me.

I looked round. The floor was covered in a resilient material. A weight-training machine stood in one corner and some free weights. A small circular trampoline, a variable treadmill, and an exercise bike occupied a second corner, and slightly over half was empty. The lighting was indirect and very good.

Charlie McIntyre, Alf Turner, and Gordon McLeod came in together and sat on one of the two low benches. They stood as Mr Buchanan and the Duke entered.

"Sit, please," Mr Buchanan said. "We all know each other, although one hasn't served with us before. We are now operational."

He pointed at each in turn, and each responded with his name.

"Alf."

"Gordon."

"Charlie."

"Gerry."

"Peter, you all know, and me, Murdoch."

Alf raised a finger.

"Yes, Alf?"

"Are we official this time out, Murdoch?"

"No. Do you want out?"

"No, just wanted to know. That's all."

I cleared my throat and they all looked at me.

"Uncle Gerry," I said, and the Duke made the chopping motion with his right hand.

"Gerry is fine with this group, in private session, Peter."

Alf Turner looked from me to the Duke with a broad grin then whistled softly.

"I want to know what this is all about," I said.

Mr Buchanan cleared his throat.

"Neil Campbell has jumped bail, and, we hear, threatens to kill you. I feel some responsibility as I didn't realise in time the potential of your group. We intend to make sure nothing happens to you or the others."

"Neil Campbell is not to be killed," I said, "nor is anyone he might send against us if it can possibly be avoided."

"Is that the Royal We, My Lord of Möbius?" The Duke grinned.

Mr Buchanan laughed as I moved my right hand up and down, heel down.

"I am not joking. No, Gerry, it is us, The Group. He is to be found and turned over to the police. There is to be no unnecessary killing. Is that understood?"

"Agreed," they said in turn.

Suddenly embarrassed, and a boy again, I blushed.

Charlie nodded at me then said: "I'm much happier about training now, Murdoch. You've done well."

"Peter's done well," Mr Buchanan said.

Talk turned to practical matters and we broke up shortly before nine. Alf would coordinate security between his group and Gordon McLeod's, and the Duke would fund a private agency to help trace Campbell. Charlie would get us boys started on our training.

"Where have you two been?" Davey said as Mr Buchanan and I came in.

"Out," I said.

"Joan thought her dad had scared you off," Davey said. "She really laughed when I told her about your bed on Saturday night, didn't she, Mike?"

On the way home I told Davey about the gym.

 **Twenty Six**

"I thought this would be fun." Davey groaned, and dropped to do push-ups.

"Shut up and get going, Davey," Alf Turner said.

We had been training for two weeks. Alf Turner and Gordon McLeod from the school had us working out with weights and exercises.

"Your endurance capacity isn't bad at all," Gordon told us when we came back from a run together. "Much better than most modern youths, but we need some upper body muscle."

"Mr McLeod," Davey said, "Alf says you have to learn to use an opponent's strength against him. Why do you say we have to build up muscle?"

"You're lazy, Davey. Alf's right, of course a really skilled and trained weak person can beat an untrained or poorly trained stronger man or woman. What happens if you bump into someone who's both strong and trained?"

"Will we get muscles like the photos in the mags, like those three sixth formers that do all the weight-training?" Davey said.

"And all the posing?" I said.

"Not if I can help it, you won't. You'll have some muscle to show for sure. What we want to do is develop upper body strength and endurance, with the emphasis on endurance. Now get on with Alf's push-ups and less chat."

When Charlie appeared at the door communicating with Mr Buchanan's shop, Davey seized the chance to stop the exercise he was working on and dash over to him.

"I'm bushed, Charlie. I won't have any energy left for your lessons, by the time Alf and Mr McLeod are finished with us."

"Go and fetch the packages out of my car, and stop grumbling."

Charlie took a pretend swing at Davey, who ducked and ran out.

Mike was already more muscular than me and was more solidly built to start with. Charlie scanned him appraisingly.

"You are going to be a powerful man when you're full grown, Mike. A regular blacksmith."

Mike grinned and flexed his arm.

"Remember, Alf, they're still only boys. Watch they don't get over extended. Growing muscles and joints can be damaged."

"Yes, Mother Hen." Alf grinned. "You're getting soft in your old age. I wish you'd been half so considerate when you trained me."

"You're tough as nails, Alf, and always were. You're as big a dodger as Davey."

Davey struggled in with a cardboard box half a head bigger than him. He put it down and puffed.

"There's still another box in the car."

"Yes," Charlie said, "bring it in too."

With a scowl at Mike and me, Davey left again, grumbling under his breath.

Both boxes in the centre of the floor, Charlie said: "Right Davey, open them up."

"Why me?"

"Because, knowing you, you're the one who still needs the exercise. Now do it."

The long box had four staves about an inch and a half thick and five feet long. The surface of each staff was slightly roughened. Davey reached to pick one up to play with it.

Charlie said: "Get the rest out first."

The rest was four swords and four daggers.

"Mr Buchanan said swords like these were worn by knights and gentry in the twelfth century, not the great two-handed broadswords," Charlie said. "These have the right heft to them. Yours is the slightly smaller one, Davey."

Davey touched an edge.

"They're blunt."

"You don't think I'd trust you three with sharp implements, do you?" Charlie said. "Swords of that day were for slashing, hacking, and jabbing. None of the ballet style fencing you see in movies or on TV. Those are copies of authentic practice weapons."

Davey pirouetted round and made a jab at Charlie, who moved quickly, and the sword clattered to the floor.

"Ow, that hurt," Davey exclaimed, and rubbed his wrist.

Charlie cuffed Davey.

"Blunt or not, these are still weapons. Don't ever point a weapon at any of us again, unless you mean business, or we've agreed to practice."

"But–"

"But nothing, Davey. Don't do it. Clear?"

"Yes, I suppose. You hurt my wrist, Charlie."

Without answer, Charlie sat on a bench and pulled Davey across his knee. Davey kicked and struggled, and Charlie gave him three hard whacks on his rump with the flat of a sword.

"Ow. What was that for?"

"If I'm weapon training you, you do what you're told, when you're told. Clear?"

Davey scowled and rubbed his rear.

"Yes, I–"

He stopped and grinned.

"Yes, Charlie, sir."

Alf put an arm round Davey's shoulder and shook him.

"His bark's worse than his bite. He terrified me when I was in training."

"If that's him barking, I don't want to be around when he bites."

"The other box, Davey," Charlie said, and Davey leapt into action.

This time he unpacked padded jackets and gauntlets, heavily padded on the back, and thin leather on the palm side. Helmets with visors were next and finally eight long round pads.

"What are these for? There's a hole up the middle of the length of them," Davey held one up and peered into it, "but it doesn't go all the way through."

The pads fitted on each end of each quarter-staff. Alf threw a staff to Davey, picked one up himself, and stood in front of Davey, staff held lightly in both hands.

"Right, Davey, defend yourself. This is what you've been waiting for."

Davey copied Alf's stance. He successfully parried a couple of jabs and swings, then with a broad grin said: "This is easy."

The jab to his midriff surprised and winded him, and Alf's swing to his head knocked Davey off his feet. His staff spun out of his grasp and Davey glared up at Alf standing over him.

"Easy is it, Davey?"

Alf prodded Davey with the staff. Davey grabbed the staff, and pulled hard, and at the same time kicked up hard. Alf fell writhing, and in an instant Davey squirmed astride him, Alf's staff pressed down hard on his throat. Gordon McLeod pulled Davey to his feet and away, and placed himself between Alf and Davey.

"Murdoch. Get in here. Now!" Charlie called from the doorway.

"What's the problem?"

"Your boys. I've had enough of this mystery. They're dangerous enough without being taught to fight. What are we training them for? A year ago they were ordinary boys, a bit soft if anything, by all accounts. Look at them now. They're not soft; mentally or physically. The Campbells learned that. Davey's reaction was not that of a thirteen-year-old innocent of our time. Alf's little joke could have cost him his life."

"I'm sorry, Alf," Davey said, and peered out from behind Gordon McLeod.

"It's all right. Try to remember whose side I'm on. OK? Let him go, Gordon. It was as much my fault as Davey's."

Hesitantly, Davey took Alf's hand and they shook.

"That's it for me for today, lads," Alf said. "Come on, Davey, I'll treat you to an ice cream."

"Hold it," Charlie said, "that's exactly what I mean. One minute they're boys," he smiled. "Rather nice boys, but something happens, and *bang* they're a hit team. A thoroughly dangerous team, not under any proper control."

"That's why we have to train them."

"Come clean, Murdoch. What's going on? What is the Duke's stake in all this? I've never known him to take any real interest in this island beyond his revenues. Certainly not in any boys outside his own family."

Mr Buchanan turned to me, one eyebrow raised. "It's your story, Peter, but the group does work better without secrets from each other."

"I'll never remember who knows and who doesn't," Davey grumbled.

I told them the short version of our year in the past and watched their faces intently.

Alf Turner listened impassively and when I finished said: "That's it? Nothing's changed. Come on, Davey, let's go for the ice cream."

He and Davey left arm in arm.

Gordon McLeod's face glowed.

"What an adventure. God, what an adventure."

Charlie McIntyre frowned, gnawed at his lower lip, then his face became red and he scowled.

"This is insanity, Murdoch. You've let your own biases warp your judgment. We should be bringing these boys down, not training them. They have to live in this society. What we are about to do is totally inappropriate."

"Now hold hard there, Charlie. Hear me out. I did start to debrief them and started to bring them down, but there's something else to consider. What if the boys want to go back?"

"I would not encourage them."

"Charlie, you know me. I wouldn't try to influence Peter or Michael, but the complication is that they might not have a choice. Peter is linked to that time, and through him, so are Michael and Davey. I've read the private history of the Duke's family. It seems to me as if they do or did go back. Would you let them go back to the twelfth century without our skills? Would you have that on your conscience?"

"Don't try to softsoap me, Murdoch. They survived the year by Peter's account, didn't they?"

"Yes, but when, if, they go back, this time it'll be different. They killed the Duke, remember? They have enemies there now. They swore to defend the Duke's son during his minority."

"Yes, I suppose so, but–"

"Charlie. The Duke's private records talk about Davey, Master of the Demon Skin; Peter, Lord of Möbius; the Brothers of Keith the Cripple. Peter didn't know any of that from the records. Those records are authentic, I'd swear to it. The Masters of Möbius vanished for a year after the Duke's death, then reappeared when the infant duke and his mother were in trouble. The Duke now is concerned that, if the boys don't go back, history will somehow change."

"Enough, Murdoch. Pete, what do you think?"

"I don't know. Sometimes I think I would like to go back, but I don't want to drag Mike and Davey along if they don't want to go. Mr Buchanan's idea that we might not have a choice hadn't struck me."

"Let's get this settled, Charlie," Mr Buchanan said. "Given that it's happened before, do you agree it would be criminal of us not to prepare the boys to survive?"

Charlie held up his hands.

"Murdoch, you could have been the Black Pope. I'll train the boys till August, just in case. If they are still here after that, and I pray God they will be, then we have a solemn duty to be equally devoted to teaching them to live at peace in this time."

Twenty Seven

"Two letters for you today, Peter," Aunt Jean called when we clattered in from school.

"Want something to eat to keep us going till tea?" Davey said, while we changed.

"No. You go."

Throwing myself on my bed, I studied the two envelopes.

Which should I open first?

Eventually I put Mom's letter on the pillow and opened Dad's.

After washing my face, I peered at myself in the mirror.

My eyes do look a bit red, but maybe no one will notice.

"What did your mum and dad say?" Davey said when I came down.

"Leave Peter be. He'll tell us if he feels like it. Have some milk and a biscuit, Peter. Tea will be a little late. Uncle Alex's stocktaking. Not you, Davey. You've had your biscuit. Have an apple if you're still hungry."

While I screened the biscuit tin from his mother, Davey snatched one and left saying: "I'm off to do my homework."

I sat at the kitchen table. "Mom and Dad are both coming over for Christmas."

"I know. Your mum wrote to me too. She'll stay here."

"Dad's going to stay with Aunt Ina. He says I'm to move in there with him."

"Your mum's expecting you to spend some time with your dad, but I don't think she thought you'd spend the whole time with him."

"What do I do, Aunt Jean? I know Mom's looking forward to me being here, but she doesn't mind if I spend some time with Dad. If she can understand, why can't Dad?"

At night after Davey was asleep, I crept down to the lounge. As I hoped, Grandpa sat there in the dark, at the window which faced out to the sea.

Without turning round, Grandpa said: "That you, Peter? Come on in. It's been a while since we talked."

We gossiped for a while about school and our training, and laughed over some of Davey's antics. For a short time we sat in a companionable silence, then I started to tell Grandpa about the letters and my dilemma. In the dim light from the street lamp outside, I thought Grandpa's face changed colour. His hand went to clutch at his throat.

"Peter, quick. My pills ... they're on the–"

I ran and was back in seconds. I opened the pill box and without waiting to be told, popped one into Grandpa's open mouth. Grandpa grasped my hand in a crushing grip, and I sank to my knees beside the chair.

The breathing eased and the grip slackened.

"Should I get Uncle Alex or Aunt Jean?"

"No. I'm fine now. Let's not disturb them."

"Can I help you to bed then?"

"No, Peter. I'm better off sitting up. That's why Alex and Jean got me this chair. I'm going to take another pill, and sit here with my eyes closed."

I sat on the floor beside the chair, and took Grandpa's hand again. I woke with a start, my arm cramped.

Was Grandpa dead?

I moved, and Grandpa said: "I must have dropped off. You still here, Peter? Off to bed with you."

Twenty Eight

Mom and Dad were due to arrive on the afternoon ferry on the Sunday after school closed. I served Mass for Charlie, as I now did most Sundays, and went to Aunt Ina's for brunch.

She was all bright and chatty. "I thought you'd have all your stuff with you. Well, never mind, we can pick it up after we meet your dad. I've put an extra bed in your old room for you, and your dad can have the big bed."

"Mum will be on the same ferry. I'll be going home with her. I'll be half time here and half time at the Lamonts'."

"That's not what your dad and I intend, Peter. Now your father's here we will see a change."

"Ina, for Heaven's sake, you make every meeting a confrontation. I'm amazed that Pete still comes."

"Don't blaspheme, John. It's Peter. I'm tired telling you that Pete is common."

"His friends call him Pete."

"You're not even a blood relative, and you are much too old to be his friend."

"John is a friend."

"Be respectful. It's Uncle John to you, young man."

"John is fine, Pete."

"Another friend once said, 'We may chose our friends, but God gave our relations'."

"I said that to you, Peter. I am pleased you now classify me a friend."

Uncle John laughed. "Ina, you are a glutton for punishment if you still want him with the Jesuits. A triumph of faith and hope over observed reality."

Aunt Ina sniffed and maintained a frosty silence till we set out for the harbour. I walked beside Uncle John and took his arm. "If you must take someone's arm, Peter, come to this side and take mine."

Uncle John squeezed my arm and, with a sigh, let go and moved over to beside Aunt Ina.

The Lamonts were already at the harbour and Davey ran over to join me.

"Hello, Mr Calder, Mrs Calder," Davey said. "Pete, we moved one of the beds out of our room down to Grandpa's. Your mom will use our room and we'll sleep in Grandpa's."

I made to move to join the Lamonts and Aunt Ina hissed: "Peter Macdonald, you stay right here."

Just then, Charlie appeared. He greeted the Calders then said: "Might I have a word with Pete?"

Without waiting for an answer, he took me by the arm and led me to a position half way between the Calders and the Lamonts.

"Neutral ground, Pete. Okay?"

Relieved, I grinned and we stood in a friendly silence till the ferry docked.

"Oh, oh. They're putting on two gangways, one fore and one aft," Charlie said, and I started to look from one gangway to the other, hoping against hope my parents would come down the same gangway, together.

I spotted my mother on the fore gangway and set off at a run. Aunt Ina shouted and waved.

"There's your dad." She pointed to the aft gangway. I reached my mother as she stepped ashore. I threw myself into her arms, hugged and hugging.

"My, how you've grown, Peter. I'm glad you weren't too big for a hug."

The Lamonts all rushed up and Mom swatted me on the bottom.

"Go and meet your dad, Peter."

When I ran back down the pier I skidded to a standstill short of Dad and the Calders.

"About time, Peter," Aunt Ina said.

"Shut up, Ina," Uncle John snapped.

Dad put out his hand and I made to shake hands. Uncle John gave me a push between my shoulder blades, to send me stumbling into Dad's arms.

The Lamonts had already started up the sea front towards their house and I was torn between walking with Mom or Dad.

"Catch up on your mother," Uncle John said. "Phone us later about the times you'll be staying with us."

"Right, Uncle John. See you later, Dad."

Running off, I heard Dad's voice say: "I thought I gave instructions he was to stay with us?"

The report cards arrived on the Tuesday, Christmas Eve. To my delight I was first in the class. Mom was very pleased for me; so were the Lamonts. I was worried Davey might be upset at his parents' pleasure over my results, but he shrugged.

"That's great, Pete. We can't all be first. It'll take the spotlight off my report."

That evening, I was due at the Calders' to spend time with Dad, and I took the report with me. After tea we talked generally and had a very pleasant time. Not as free and relaxed as with the Lamonts, but good nonetheless.

"My report card came in today. Would you like to see it?"

Uncle John agreed enthusiastically. Dad less so, I thought.

It was passed from Dad to Aunt Ina and then to Uncle John in silence.

Uncle John read it through and said: "Great work, Pete, congratulations. I'm proud of you."

"No more than I would expect," Dad said. "You've had the advantage of a very expensive education in the States. I'd have been disappointed if you couldn't beat the children here in the local council school."

"Is that all you've got to say, you great gowk?" Uncle John said, after a glance at my face. "Pete's worked hard after having missed a year. I'm proud of him."

"It doesn't matter, John. Let me have the report please."

"It is Uncle John to you, Peter," Dad said. "You will be calling your aunt and I by our first names next."

"No he won't," Uncle John said. "Pete's very picky about his friends."

There was a deathly silence, then Uncle John rose and left the room. Minutes later, the front door slammed.

"Extraordinary behaviour," Dad said, shaking his head. "Well, never mind. I shall keep the report card. I'm going over to St Martin's in a day or so to see the Rector. You will be there till the summer, and I will arrange a good boarding school in the States for next year."

Aunt Ina nodded approvingly, and smiled grimly when I made no direct reply.

"I'm serving at midnight Mass, Dad. I've got to be there about eleven fifteen."

"Good boy, Peter. I am pleased that despite influences to the contrary you have kept up your observances. I'll walk with you. A little quiet contemplation will do me good."

At the church, I sought Charlie out and told him the tale of my evening.

"Can Dad do this?"

"I don't know, but I'll find out."

While I served, I glanced out over the congregation. Uncle John and Aunt Ina sat beside each other, but not together. Uncle John winked. On the other side of the aisle I saw Mom and, to my surprise, Aunt Jean and Davey. Davey grinned and waved.

After the service, Charlie did not stay to joke with the boys, and I wondered where he had gone. When I came out onto the steps of the church, Charlie was there, talking to Mom and Dad.

"Merry Christmas, Mom."

"Merry Christmas, Peter."

"Kiss your mother, Peter, and let's go," Dad said.

On our walk to the Calders', Dad fumed.

"That curate had the effrontery to take your mother and I to task over our treatment of you. He wants us to meet at the Rectory on Friday."

"And will you?"

"Yes, I suppose we will, but counselling is not the answer. Your mother simply has to come to her senses."

On Friday, I was due to move back in with the Lamonts. I felt very welcome.

"Who will be at the meeting today, Mom?" I said.

"Well, your dad and I. Jean and Alex Lamont have been asked to come, so I suppose John and Ina Calder will be there too."

At the Rectory, Charlie showed us into a large room with a big table.

"Please take a seat. Pete, will you help me with the tea, please?"

When Charlie and I carried the tea in, Mom and Dad were on either side of the table. Aunt Ina sat with Dad, and Aunt Jean and Uncle Alex with Mom. Charlie frowned.

"Will you sit down too, Mr Calder?" Charlie said, and Uncle John nodded.

"Where are you sitting, Pete? I'll sit with you."

"Pete and I will sit at the end, Mr Calder."

There was an empty chair beside me and Uncle John sat there, which placed him on the same side of the table as the Lamonts. Aunt Ina scowled, but Uncle John nodded at Alex beside him.

"Is there any possibility of a reconciliation?" Charlie said.

"I am only too prepared to have Helen back, if she comes to her senses."

"I said a reconciliation, not an unconditional surrender, Mr Macdonald."

There was an uncomfortable silence.

Charlie cleared his throat.

"My concern is for Pete and his welfare. Can you two adults chose another battleground? This is very destructive to Pete. He should not be forced to choose between you, but in the circumstances, his rights and feelings must be protected."

Several people started to talk at once. Over the noise I heard the doorbell.

"Get the door, Pete, please," Charlie said.

I came back in with the Duke and a stranger.

"I took the liberty of inviting these gentlemen," Charlie said, and introduced the Duke to the others.

Seated, the Duke said: "This is Mr McCallum. He is Peter's solicitor. He will instruct counsel in any court challenge."

"Peter has no such rights," Dad burst out.

Mr McCallum peered at Dad over his half spectacles.

"In general no, Mr Macdonald, unless abuse is suspected. However, when you or Mrs Macdonald apply to a court for custody, my client, at fourteen, is entitled to be heard and represented by counsel."

"That is very expensive," Aunt Ina said, and smiled. "Peter's mother could not afford such services for very long."

The Duke shrugged. "This does not involve Mrs Macdonald. Peter has enough credit to retain Mr McCallum, and the very best available counsel. Certainly until his majority."

Dad spluttered. "What business is this of yours, sir?"

He glowered at the Duke.

The Duke shrugged. "Your wife's family and mine are interrelated over the centuries."

Everyone was so intent on the drama between the Duke and Dad that no one noticed me slip out.

Twenty Nine

Too angry to cry, I peddled hard on Davey's cycle. I took it and rode off with no destination in mind. Now, when I looked round me, I was on the road that followed the old monastery trail. Why not?

When the road turned away from the old trail, I lifted the bicycle over the drystone dyke and started to walk. It was fully dark before I reached the ruins and a fine drizzle froze as it fell. I shivered.

Where would the chapel have been?

I attempted to orient myself, and everything wavered and shadows moved. The shadows solidified.

I was in the Abbey chapel. A door opened and there was the soft flip-flop of the sandals the monks wore, and the thud of wood on stone slab. Flickering shadows moved on the floor. Two figures, one carrying a staff.

I turned to face the door — one of the figures was Keith. The boy who had gone with us into the past a year ago. Crippled there, he had chosen to stay. Bernard, who had deserted the Duke's service to look after Keith, was at his side.

Keith hobbled forward, leaning on his staff, and I threw my arms round him. When we stepped apart, Bernard bowed. "Welcome, Master Peter."

He hesitated for an instant, then I put my arms out to him. We embraced, and Bernard patted my back. "Sit down, masters. Here on the bench in the niche."

We talked of the others from both times, both intent on filling the gap since we last met. Keith reported that the infant duke's mother was strong-willed and capable, but there were problems.

"The young duke needs My Lord of Möbius and his brothers," Bernard said. "Andrew says we should not expect you until the time of the Hunt, if then."

"Keith, I'm better here. Back in our time I cause trouble for everyone. Uncle John and Aunt Ina were fine till I appeared. Mike's dad and his group were settled to live a quiet comfortable life, in a small town. I've got them all stirred up. Mom has her practice and clients to think of, and her mind is more with them than me. Dad thinks he wants what's best for me, but he really wants to relive life through me, to own me. I should have stayed where – when – I was needed."

"I don't understand all that, Pete, but I'm glad I didn't go back. The Abbot will accept me as a postulant in January."

We sat for a short time in silence, each lost in his own thoughts. A bell tolled.

"We must take our place with the other lay brothers, master," Bernard said. "Will you wait in the visitors' alcove, Master Peter, or would you meet the Abbot first?"

I shook my head, but when Keith and Bernard left, I turned to the altar instead of the visitors' alcove. I knelt, but didn't hear the brothers process in.

From a long way off I heard voices.

"Mike, run and open the door. I can manage him."

"Good God. What's happened? Is that Peter?"

"He's not hurt. Hypothermia, I think, Mrs B. We've got to get him warmed up."

"Right, Michael's room. He's like ice. Turn the blanket on, Michael. Pull off the wet outer clothes and his shoes and socks. Right, cover him. That's right, Michael, tuck him in."

"I'll phone the Lamonts and the Calders."

"Good, Mr Turner, and Father McIntyre at the Rectory. Murdoch has gone out along the beach."

I opened my eyes. I was in Mike's bed. Mrs Buchanan held my wrist.

"Hello, you're with us again, are you?"

"Hi, Mrs Buchanan."

"I'll *hi* you, Peter Macdonald. What a fright you've given everyone!"

"Are you all right, Pete?" Mike sat on the other side of the bed.

"Yes, thanks, Mike. What happened?"

"I've phoned, Mrs B. They're all on their way. Alex Lamont has sent Davey out along the beach to find Mr Buchanan. Oh. You're awake, Pete."

"Yes, Alf. Thanks."

Alf motioned Mrs Buchanan to step away from the bed out of earshot, and in a low voice not intended for me, said: "Is he okay? It was more like a seizure to me than anything else. He was flat out on his face, arms stretched out to each side. If this hadn't been under his cheek, he'd have been frozen to the slab."

There was an uproar downstairs and Mike's room was full of people.

"Quiet," Mrs Buchanan bellowed, and continued in the startled silence: "Peter is fine. Now, everybody out. Downstairs. Jean, will you make tea for everyone? Mrs Calder, perhaps you could help with some sandwiches? There's cake and biscuits in the tins. Everybody out, except you, Mr Turner. I'll let you know when you can see him."

From the top of the stairs, Mrs Buchanan shouted down: "Mr Lamont, Senior. No one up here till I say. Right?"

Grandpa's voice sounded: "Right, Helen. I'll keep the gate."

"Now, Mr Turner, help me undress him. He should be a bit warmer now."

"I can undress myself," I protested.

"Shut up and do as you're told, Pete. Mrs B's in charge."

In no time they had me stripped and Mrs Buchanan went over every inch of my skin quickly but thoroughly.

"No damage, hands and feet a bit red. Mr Turner, there should be pyjamas in that top drawer. You, lie still, I've seen naked boys before. Fine. Mr Turner, slip them on and get him tucked up again."

The door opened and Mrs Buchanan turned to bellow, but stopped short when Grandpa came in with a tray.

"Hot tea, strong enough to stand a spoon up in, and plenty of sugar. Michael's on guard."

Alf darted to take the tray and Mrs Buchanan took Grandpa's arm.

"I'm fine, Helen, fine."

Alf had placed a chair beside the bed and they seated Grandpa there. I tried to sit up, but I felt weak and faint. Alf helped, then held me while Mrs Buchanan arranged the pillows.

"Right, drink some of this."

After the tea and some dry biscuits, I felt much better. Mrs Buchanan left to see to her guests.

"I'm sorry, Grandpa. I didn't mean to cause all this fuss. I wanted to be on my own and think."

Alf had withdrawn to the window and I introduced him.

"Things sure pop and sizzle when your grandson is around, sir."

"How did you come to find him, Mr Turner?"

"It was Mike really. The others were searching all over, close to town, at places Mike and Davey had suggested. Mike suddenly asked, 'Can your four wheel drive go right up to the monastery ruins?' and off we went."

"Did you get Davey's bike?" I said.

"Yes, we brought it back with you."

"What did you see?" I said.

"You flat out on your face. Very difficult it was too in the dark."

"Tell me the truth, Alf. What did you see?"

"What makes you think I saw anything?"

"Alf, you're not crazy. Don't worry about Grandpa. Now, what did you see?"

Alf swallowed, then grinned.

"When we got there, nothing. I would swear there was nothing there. Then suddenly, you were there on your face, like I said."

"Alf."

"Well, it was dark remember, very dark."

"If you're not going to trust me, Alf, I don't need you. You may leave us."

"Peter. Don't be so rude. Mr Turner may have saved your life."

"No, Mr Lamont, he's right. How he knows, I don't know. He was out cold, as unconscious as any I've ever seen. All right. All right. I'm getting there," Alf said in response to an impatient scowl from me.

"When you appeared, there a young boy with a stick. About Davey's size, but thinner. A big plug-ugly with only one ear, and on his knees beside you was a well-set man."

"You saw Keith, Bernard, and the Abbot," I breathed. "I was there, Grandpa."

Alf cleared his throat and Grandpa and I looked at him.

"I heard something too. Now that it seems I wasn't dreaming or hallucinating, I'm bound by it. I rushed up to you to kneel beside you, and the boy and the kneeling man vanished. The tough looking character with one ear stayed and said: 'Take care of My Lord.' When I didn't answer immediately he clipped me one. A bleeding solid ghost! 'You will care for My Lord and guard him well.' I said I would. So we're stuck with each other, My Lord."

I put my hand out and Alf and I shook.

"I'll tell you the whole story some time. What was it you found under my cheek?"

"Oh, you heard that did you?"

From the chest of drawers Alf picked up a cloth which had been carefully folded in a square.

"It's the Abbot's stole," I said.

Mrs Buchanan allowed the others in to see me in pairs, then sent them all packing.

ⓧ Thirty

"Sit up, Peter. Breakfast."

Mrs Buchanan stood at the bedside with a tray, and Mike came in after his mother, still in his pyjamas.

"I can't remember the last time Mum gave me breakfast in bed."

"It's only tea and toast, Michael."

"Come on in, Mike," I said. "It's a double bed. There's plenty of room and plenty of toast."

"Not so fast, young man. You run downstairs and get yourself a mug."

Seated in bed, I told Mike about the meeting at the Rectory the afternoon before.

"I wasn't running away. I wanted someplace to think."

"Pete, if you were at the monastery shortly after dark, and we didn't find you till after midnight, you were out on that slab in the sleet with it freezing on you for about eight hours."

"I was with Keith and Bernard and the Abbot at first, then I fell into a sort of trance. Oh Mike. It's so difficult. I think I'm needed back then. I don't want to hurt people like Aunt Jean and Uncle Alex and Uncle John. Your mom and dad too. I can't leave Grandpa now, especially if Davey comes with me."

We sat silent, then there were voices downstairs. The door opened and Mrs Buchanan stuck her head in. "Visitors."

161

Davey bounced in. "I thought I smelled toast."

Joan followed him in.

"There's no toast left," Davey said, peering at the empty plate.

"Davey, don't you ever think of anything but your stomach? How are you, Pete? Why are you in bed with him, Mike?"

Mike and I both blushed.

"We were having breakfast."

"You certainly made a stir last night," Joan said.

"I thought nobody but us knew," I said.

"The Duke phoned Dad, after midnight. Boy, was Dad mad. His Lordship shouted at him for not having a search party out earlier. Dad shouted back. No one had informed him that 'the mystery boy was on the wander again'."

We all laughed.

"Well, I'm off then," Joan said. "I bumped into Davey in the street and he said you were here."

Mike and I dressed, then the three of us joined Mrs Buchanan in the kitchen.

"Coffee, Peter?" she said.

Davey screwed up his nose.

"I know you and Michael don't like coffee, but Peter does. You two can have tea or milk."

"And biscuits? I've been up for hours."

"A biscuit, Davey Lamont. One each, and that's it."

"What happens now, Mrs Buchanan?"

"Apparently after you left, before anyone noticed or worried about you not being there, some sort of agreement was reached. Your dad and Ina Calder shouted a lot, but as far as I can make out from Jean, the final upshot was you would be allowed to stay where you want to stay and go to the school of your choice. Your dad wasn't at all happy with it, Jean says."

"They both agreed?"

"Yes, I think so. Jean said your dad would probably have won out if the solicitor, McCallum, hadn't been there."

"Dad could have hired more lawyers and for longer than Mom could, if it came to that. She only has her salary. The money is Dad's."

"There's to be another meeting. Here at four o'clock for a final settlement."

"Why here?"

"Because I'm not letting you out of my sight today, till I'm sure you're well."

At four sharp, the Duke and Mr McCallum arrived, followed almost immediately by Dad and Aunt Ina. Mom and Aunt Jean were already there.

Dad said: "Thank you, Mrs Buchanan, for your care of Peter last night, and for letting us have this meeting here. I'm sorry to evict you from your own lounge, but we will be as brief as possible."

Mrs Buchanan flushed and rose.

Dismissed like a servant in her own house.

Red-faced, I pushed her back into her chair and sat on the arm with a hand on her shoulder.

"Mrs Buchanan stays. To me, she's family."

I turned and kissed her cheek.

"Right, Aunt Helen?" She flushed again and patted my knee.

"I'll get the tea ready."

"Later," I said.

McCallum cleared his throat, and glanced at the Duke, who nodded.

"I have here a memorandum of agreement between Peter Roderick Macdonald, resident of the State of Maine, in the United States of America, and Helen Macdonald, nee…"

"Get on with the meat of it, McCallum. Never mind the legal verbiage."

"I was omitting the legal language, My Lord. In essence, the party of the first part, namely–"

The Duke growled something, and I laughed when I spotted the chopping gesture before the Duke said: "The long and the short of it is Peter's mother and father agree that Peter may remain here if he chooses, attend the school of his choice, and they will accept his choice of guardian, within some limits. Peter, is this agreeable to you?"

I nodded.

"Sit down, McCallum, and get Peter's choices recorded. Let's get this agreement signed."

"Is Mr McCallum truly my solicitor, Uncle Gerry?" I said, and Dad's eyes snapped wide open and he glared from me to the Duke.

"Yes, he is."

"Mr McCallum, will you join me in the dining room? I would like a private word."

"*Touché*, My Lord," McCallum said, with a smile at the Duke.

When McCallum and I re-entered, the Duke was drumming his fingers on the arm of the chair. The only sound in a silence that could be felt.

"My Lord, Ladies,"

"Let Peter tell us, McCallum, if you have no objections that is, Peter."

"I will stay on the island and attend the local school. If they will have me, I will stay with the Lamonts."

I paused and turned to Aunt Jean, and smiled back at her when she nodded.

"Mr McCallum informs me I need not name a guardian, but I prefer to do so. My guardian will be Gerald, Duke of This Island and the Lands Beyond."

"Thank you, Peter. I have tried to keep quiet and not to interfere. A very clever choice. See how pleased our descendant is. He thinks it's him."

McCallum passed the document to Dad, who read it and signed.

"I do this under protest. Someone has had undue and improper influence over my son. I see no reason to support him if he does not follow my wishes."

The Duke smiled. "No matter. Peter has funds of his own which McCallum and I will administer for him. I am very glad Peter takes after our side of the family and not yours."

The signing complete, there was another uncomfortable silence.

"Until Mom and Dad go back to the States, I will stay here with the Buchanans. I can visit both of them that way."

Dad said: "I don't care if–" but was interrupted by Aunt Ina.

"That is a very sensible suggestion, Peter. We will look forward to your visits. Won't we, Peter?"

She gave Dad one of her Medusa scowls.

"Mr McCallum is going. Can my driver drop both you and him off?" the Duke said.

When Aunt Ina and Dad had gone, the Duke grinned.

"Now what about that tea, Mrs Buchanan? Perhaps some biscuits if Davey hasn't cleaned you out."

That evening, Mr Buchanan called a meeting of The Group in his home.

"Alf, you and Gordon were supposed to be coordinating security. How in hell could Peter walk out like that? Where was your man?"

"I didn't know I was being watched," I said.

"Back off, Murdoch. You know fine Campbell was off the streets by noon yesterday." Alf laughed. "Found wandering around, drunk as a lord, begging your pardon, Gerry, right in front

165

of the police station. They couldn't miss him. 'Drunk and very disorderly.' Very neatly done."

"I know all that."

"Right then. Inspector Cameron pulled his man off when he heard. Overtime costs, remember? Our man sloped off when the word got to him. I've already had words with him about that, but if I'd been asked, I'd have told him to knock off."

"I said I didn't know I was being watched," I protested. "Why wasn't I told?"

I was present, but not the other two boys. Mr Buchanan, after a quick glance at the others, cleared his throat.

"My decision, Peter. With Campbell threatening to get you and jumping bail…"

"I knew that. I should have been told."

Mr Buchanan shrugged. "Sorry, but it's been done now."

Alf turned to me and said quietly: "Remember what was said last night? What we talked about?"

"Yes, all of it."

"Gentlemen," Alf said, raising his voice. "We each have our speciality. In the group, we each do what we're best at. The specialist runs the show, regardless of rank, when his speciality is up front, but we do have a coordinator. He arbitrates. His decision is final. He gives the orders when a committee won't do."

"Are you running for office?" Gordon laughed.

"No. We've all worked with Murdoch before. He called us out this time. Right from day one there was no question of who was in the chair."

"Do you want me to step down, Alf?" Mr Buchanan said. "I will if the group thinks I should. This would be a safe time to change."

"Spit it out, Alf," Charlie said. "What's your problem? Murdoch is the most experienced. He trained all of us."

Alf squirmed.

"Something happened last night that changed the situation for me. I'm Peter's man now."

I jumped, but Mr Buchanan put a hand on my shoulder.

"That's fine by me, Alf. So am I, and so, I think, are the others."

His eyes swept from one to another, and they nodded; Charlie after a slight hesitation.

"But we have to leave him some time to be a boy," Charlie said.

"Yes, but we're like a regency council. We are the adults. We train him, but we can't forget who and what he is," Mr Buchanan concluded.

"I don't want this," I whispered.

 **Thirty One**

The remaining days of Mom and Dad's vacation passed quickly. It was clear there was no hope of a reconciliation. When I tried to raise the subject with Mom, she ruffled my hair and said: "It's like your friend Father McIntyre said, your dad wants a total unconditional surrender, not a negotiated peace. I won't go back to being a doormat." She hugged me. "Don't blame yourself, Peter. You were simply convenient to fight over; a focus. I'm sorry."

With Dad it was even worse.

"It's none of your business, Peter. All that's needed is for your mother to come to her senses and come back. Everything will be like before."

I decided it was indeed nothing to do with me, and my agonising over it would affect nothing. I enjoyed being with both of them. Mom was more fun to be with, but Dad, since the confrontation, treated me more as an adult, and I enjoyed the grown-up conversations on all sorts of topics.

I was a little disappointed at how quiet it was at the Buchanans' on New Year's Eve. Mrs Buchanan bustled round cleaning, and insisted everyone had a bath and changed to the skin before midnight.

"In the States, we always had a party at New Year," I said, when I sat in the living room shortly before midnight.

"It's not New Year till midnight," Mike sounded puzzled.

At midnight, the church bells rang and the ships in the harbour sounded their sirens and horns. Mr and Mrs Buchanan shook hands and kissed. Then she kissed and hugged both of us. Mr Buchanan poured us each a small glass of green ginger wine and we toasted the New Year. It was very pleasant, I thought, very much at home with the Buchanans, but not exciting the way I had expected it to be.

About twelve thirty, I was about to suggest I would go to bed when the Lamonts arrived. Davey made straight for the plate of shortbread, only to be intercepted by Mrs Buchanan.

"At least wish us a Good New Year, Davey Lamont, before you eat us out of house and home," she said and kissed him.

By one, several of the Buchanans' neighbours were in, and Alf arrived with Gordon McLeod and his wife.

"Peter, why don't you go round and first foot the Calders and wish your dad a happy new year," Mom suggested.

"Can Mike and Davey come too?"

We excused ourselves and ran whooping down to the front and then to the Calders'.

To my surprise, Charlie was there and several of the parishioners.

"The Court of the Dragon Lady," Charlie whispered to me, and laughed.

We pushed through to greet Aunt Ina, Uncle John, and Dad. To my intense annoyance Dad's first words were: "I don't know what Helen and the Lamonts are thinking of, letting three young boys wander the island at night, this late."

In one of the sudden silences that sometimes falls on such gatherings, a voice said: "What does he think could happen to them? They're the most dangerous group on the island. The Paras wouldn't go near them without armoured back up."

I turned and met Tommy's eye. He flushed.

"A Happy New Year, Tommy," I said. "You too, Harry. Let's forget last year."

✑ Thirty Two

Two days after the New Year, Mom and Dad left for the States, and I moved back in with the Lamonts. I was sad to see them go, but in a strange sort of way relieved. It was as if one part of my life was over. I had denied to myself that the problem existed, then been self-pitying, then guilt ridden and angry by turns. Now I accepted that two people who loved me, and whom I loved, no longer loved each other, and it was not my fault or responsibility. It was simply a fact, a sad fact.

Back at school, I threw myself into my work. Since the actual schoolwork was comparatively easy for me, I pushed ahead with my maths and became engrossed with the mathematical aspects of cartography and surveying. I started to read widely on medieval fortification systems and siege techniques. The one area I had no interest in at all was computers.

Mike spent much of his leisure with Uncle John Calder at his garage. Being in a small town in a farming area, Uncle John was much more than a motor mechanic. He had a local reputation for being able to fix anything in metal and Mike pleased him by learning his skills. The speed at which Mike became proficient delighted Uncle John.

As for Davey, he continued to muddle along somewhere in the middle of the class. When Alex Lamont had taken him to task over

171

some complaint from the school, and had compared him unfavourably with me, Grandpa had stepped in.

"That'll do Alex. Leave Davey be. He's not a carbon copy of Peter, nor should he be. He's himself. In some ways he's a lot like you at his age. Not in appearance, maybe, but certainly the way I remember you."

The three of us continued to train hard in the Duke's gym. The exercises visibly strengthened our arms and shoulders. Both Alf and Charlie insisted that in fighting with swords and quarterstaffs, given two well matched opponents, endurance and stamina could well be the deciding factor. For that reason, they insisted on long bouts with few breathers.

Alf and Charlie were merciless taskmasters and nothing short of complete mastery of the skills they were teaching was acceptable. Davey, being left-handed, had a natural advantage in swordplay, or so Charlie claimed, but he made all three of us practice endlessly with both hands, switching hands in the course of a bout.

One day, the Duke announced we must learn to ride.

"Alf too," I decreed.

"Oh, no. I'll stick to my jeep," Alf said. "I don't know one end of a horse from the other, and I don't want to. I'm a town boy."

I insisted, and we started driving out to the estate to learn how to handle horses. Despite his protestations, Alf learned almost as quickly as us boys, and soon we were able to control the horse with our legs, leaving our hands free for weapons.

To everyone's surprise, his own included, Davey turned out to have a real flair for handling horses, and soon the groom was enthusiastic in his praise for Davey's progress.

"The others are passable, no more, but Davey could eventually be a real horseman."

He frowned when Alf said: "If we can control our mounts and handle our weapons without danger to our horses or ourselves, then you've done your job."

"I can't think why kids today would need such skills if they aren't getting ready for the ring."

Despite Alf's comment, he was lavish in his praise of Davey's performance and he made sure Mike and I realised how good with horses Davey was.

Secure, confident, and comfortable in the saddle, we and Alf rode regularly, but Davey, enthused, began to hang out at the estate stables. The Duke introduced him to the local veterinarian who was delighted to find a youngster really interested in horses and the larger farm animals and their problems. Davey even started taking schoolwork more seriously, at least biology.

 **Thirty Three**

With Mike and Davey now off frequently on their own interests, I spent more of my spare time with Charlie, Mr Buchanan and Gordon McLeod. When Alf was not working, he was my constant companion.

One day Gordon tried to interest me in history, particularly that of the island and surrounding areas. "No way, Gordon," I said, walking away.

Later, with the group, I apologised to him.

"I'm sorry about the history, Gordon, but I've avoided reading Uncle Gerry's records too."

The Duke nodded. "I noticed that. Davey and Michael show much more interest. Why, Peter?"

"If I go back, I don't want to live out my life like an actor acting out a script. Mouthing lines someone else has written. I don't even know for sure if when – where – we were really is our past. It could be a parallel universe. Because a road is there, I don't need to follow it. If I do, I don't want to know what every step or action foreshadows. I want to be able to act as I see fit, not to fulfil a prophecy."

"Peter, the whole point in you going back is not to change history," the Duke said.

"For you, Uncle Gerry, perhaps. I thought that was your agenda."

Charlie laughed. "He's got your measure, Gerry. You don't want anything to disturb your nice comfortable life."

The Duke shrugged. "At first perhaps that was my sole motive, but I'm hooked on the boys now. If Peter wants to play it that way, it's his life. He's the boss."

"What I do want to know, is the geography of the country like the back of my hand," I said.

"The only way to do that properly is on foot," Alf said. "That way you really appreciate distances and terrain. Good Ordnance Survey maps will certainly help for areas we can't get to. You already know the island pretty well, and the three of you can certainly make your way around with little sign or sound."

"I want to know the passes; where men can walk, can ride; where a pack train can go; where wheeled carts can't go; where a body of men can move and rest unseen; where men and supplies can be landed from the sea unseen from town or castle, but close to them."

"Whoa. We're not at war with anyone, yet," Charlie said, and they all laughed, including me.

"Perhaps the boys could take a camping trip on the mainland at spring break. That's what – a week away?" Mr Buchanan said.

"Two weeks," I said. "That would be great."

Later Mr Buchanan and I sat over a cup of coffee.

"Should I go back, Major?"

"You have to think about it, and if you go, who goes with you."

"That's not fair. Why is it my decision?"

"One of the joys of leadership, I'm afraid. Your mind brought you back to this time. Your mind and the Duke's can return you. I think yours is the link. You are the navigator. He who knows the way."

 **Thirty Four**

When I broached the idea of the trip to Mike and Davey, they were enthusiastic.

"The only question," Mike said, "is where to go. The south mainland is pretty built up now, along the coast anyway. I don't think any of it is anything like it was in our Duke's time."

"The major features won't have changed; hill tops, lochs, big landmarks like that. We can go right up onto the moor."

"Would we not be better going to the north mainland? It hasn't changed in centuries. It has changed since our Duke's time maybe, because there are small villages along the coast, but reforestation must have made it much closer than the south is. Ask him, Pete."

"Can we take the horses?" Davey said. "I don't fancy all that walking."

"Spoken like a true horseman," Mike said. "Won't walk the length of himself."

"Armies, if sent against us," the Duke said, taking over, *"would come from the south, and come in boats across the main channel. As my grandfather came with his men."*

"Would they follow existing roads?" I asked aloud.

"What you call roads in your time do not exist in my domain. There are trails between settlements, passable in fair weather, drove roads over the hills where men on foot and sheep can go, but nothing wheeled."

"What about the narrows at the north end of the island?" Mike asked.

"If the tide were right, and you were bold enough, you could perhaps swim your horse across the narrows. However, the mainland there is forest to the shore, with high hills, lochs, and bogland beyond. It would take weeks to bring an army to the narrows by the mainland, if they could find their way at all. Getting them across would be even more difficult."

The Duke laughed.

"One of the hunted was once enterprising enough to steal a horse and ride to the narrows. There, he had to await a suitable tide and we found him. His boldness had amused me somewhat. We supped there while we waited for the tide. He barely made it to the middle. We almost lost the horse. It came ashore exhausted and near dead with cold, close to the fishing town. A good horse it was, too. I would have been sorry to lose it."

"What happened to the man?" Davey said.

"What of him? Had he not chosen to try, my Captain had already a post in the water for him."

"What for?" Davey said.

"To tie him to, Master Davey. At a nicely judged height. If a wind did not get up, to back up the tide, his head would be clear, barely, at high tide, as long as the sea were calm, of course."

Shivering, I opened my eyes and in my own voice said: "I'm not sure I really wanted to hear that. We will go over the main channel to the south mainland for our trip."

"That was great, Pete. Was that really our Duke?"

"That was our Duke."

I paused, listening.

"He says I stopped him before he finished the story. If the young man had survived two tides on the post he would have released him, although stealing a horse, especially one of the Duke's, was a hanging offence."

"Fat chance of surviving two tides at the narrows," Mike said. "There's always a wind or a sea running, or both."

"You'd be able to breathe between waves – for a while anyway," Davey said, "but imagine how cold you'd be when the tide went down. Remember at the bay, Pete? Maybe they'd take him in between tides, just so he didn't die of cold before the next tide."

I shivered.

"Gerald says that was a refinement he hadn't thought of. I'd just as soon not hear any more stories like that, Gerald! Let's talk about something else."

"Who will go?" Mike said.

"Just us. Just us three," Peter replied.

"Us four, if you count the Duke," Davey said grinning. "He can tell us camp fire stories."

Thirty Five

After the twenty minute ferry crossing, we looked up and down the main street of the small town.

"Where now, Pete?" Mike said.

Davey grabbed my arm. "There's an ice cream shop. Let's have one before we head out."

Laughing, we agreed.

The ferry town was only two streets deep from the shore. A ribbon of houses and small shops ran along one side of the coast road as it hugged the shore, following every contour.

About a mile and a half out of the town, we rounded a cliff which crowded the road, forcing it to dog-leg out round it. I checked my map.

"Right lads. This is where we go up."

There was a small path up the cliff, and we scrambled up in single file, on hands and knees at one or two points. At the top, the reforestation, started some twenty years before, brought the forest right to the edge of the cliff. Where we had climbed brought us to a small clearing from which a fire break trail led off into the dark wood. We moved away from the cliff edge and stopped at the beginning of the fire trail.

"We'll go up the trail for a bit and then see," Mike said.

"Hey! Who elected you boss?" Davey objected.

"Andrew did. Remember? In the forest, Mike leads," I said.

"That was back then, and on the island. This is different."

"It still holds. Mike knows more about survival outside than we do."

"This is a camping trip. I'm not having him boss me about like before."

"Who's bossing?" Mike said. "We've all learnt a lot. We're all pretty good in the forest now, but do we want a vote every step?"

"Mike leads," I said, in a flat voice. "I say so."

Davey and I stood toe to toe, facing each other. I hadn't paid attention before, as we hadn't roughhoused recently, but Davey was almost as tall as me now. Over the past few months Davey had had a growth spurt.

Davey pushed and I pushed back. We both dropped our quarterstaffs and grappled. Soon we were wrestling and I found myself hard pressed, then with a jerk, Davey threw me and was astride me. He grinned down and held my hands flat on the ground above my head.

"Give up, My Lord?"

Davey reared up on his knees and dropped back down hard on my chest, as I tried to buck him off.

"Give up, Pete?"

There was a sound off to one side and I thought Mike was coming to my aid. A shadow fell over us, then Davey gasped and collapsed across me.

I struggled to throw Davey off, but the limp form was dragged to one side. A coarse cloth dropped over my face and someone knelt astride me and pressed a quarterstaff down on my throat. The pressure increased relentlessly, and I went limp.

"Good boy," a voice said, and the pressure relaxed. "Ah've got this yin. Jist make sure ye tie the ither two good and tight."

Minutes later, I was on my face with my arms wrenched behind my back. When my hands were tied tightly, I was hauled to my feet, frog-marched a few paces, then sent sprawling on top of Mike and Davey.

Both were conscious, but Davey was very groggy.

"What happened, Mike?"

"I was busy watching you two wrestle. The next I knew, I was here, tied, with Davey lying on top of me. Then you dropped in."

Our captors stood over us and I tensed for a blow. Instead, they pulled us apart and pushed us into a line, our backs against trees.

"It's them okay," one said.

Three burly figures looked down at us. They wore woollen ski masks and all that could be seen of the faces were the eyes and the mouth slit.

"Oh, my head," Davey groaned, and wriggled his shoulders.

"Ye'll hae a bump ahin yer ear, kid. Thae scout poles of yours ur jist the job," a second voice said, and laughed.

We were roughly pulled to our feet and pushed and prodded along the fire break trail. After about half a mile or so of stumbling progress, we turned onto a narrow foot path which opened into a small clearing, to one side of which was a small wooden shack.

"It's locked, Angus," one said, trying the door.

"Nae names, ye gormless bugger. There's a trick tae it."

The one addressed as Angus fiddled with the door and it opened. He looked inside.

"Okay, tie their feet."

We were thrown to the ground again and our feet bound at the ankles.

"Check their hauns again."

"Should we gag them, Angus?"

"For Christ's sake, we should gag ye. Naw. They'll be fine. No one ever comes up here."

They dragged us into the hut one at a time and dumped us on the floor. When the door closed we were in total darkness.

"What now, Mike?" Davey said.

"You were the one who wanted to lead."

"No I didn't, I was only arguing."

"If you hadn't been fighting Pete, those three creeps wouldn't have surprised us."

"Don't blame Davey," I said, out of the dark.

"I was just pulling his leg, Pete. Can either of you see anything?"

"Keep speaking, Mike," I said, "and we'll try to wriggle over the floor to you. Maybe we can untie each other."

Davey and I collided.

"Hey, watch where you're putting your hands, Pete,." Davey giggled.

Mike laughed. "When you two are quite finished would you try to untie each other?"

Eventually, we managed to sit in a triangle back to back, and worked on each other's bindings, but our captors had been too thorough.

Hours later, the door opened and we blinked in the sudden light.

"Is that them, Ted? Is that the buggers that did for Murray and Donald?"

"Aye, Pa. That's them."

"Help Frank pull them out."

Eyes adjusting to the light I saw there were two men with Ted. One of them was Neil Campbell.

Frank and Ted dumped us like sacks of potatoes.

"There's damn a' in their packs, Neil," Frank said.

Neil Campbell picked up one of the quarterstaffs and hefted it.

"Ye took some damn fool lessons in fightin' wi' these sticks, didn't ye? Frae the auld man at the school that died last year?"

"Aye, Pa."

Prodding each of us in turn with the staff, Neil Campbell said: "Ye're carryin' these. Fancy yersels as fighters do ye?"

He came back to Davey.

"Untie that yin, Ted." He pointed to Davey.

Davey sat up and rubbed circulation into his hands and feet.

"Let's see ye fight that yin. Show us whit ye learned. We'll watch the show. Ah'll tell ye when tae stop."

Neil Campbell handed Davey and Ted a quarterstaff each and they stood facing each other in the *en garde* position.

It was apparent to both boys that the other did know how to handle a staff. They circled cautiously and tested each other's defences.

"Come on, Ted. Stop dancin' wi' him. Knock him down and pound him. Let's have some blood."

Ted glanced quickly at his father and Davey moved. His jab got through. The abortive return stroke he parried easily and swung hard at Ted's legs, to connect below the knee with a resounding crack and a yelp from Ted. Dropping to one knee, Ted tried to block Davey's swing, but was too slow and sprawled on his back, his staff flying out of his hands.

With a shout, Davey pounced, staff swinging.

I called out: "Don't, Davey. Enough!"

Davey hesitated, and after a quick look round at Mike and me, he ran.

"After him, Frank," Neil Campbell shouted, and his friend moved off in pursuit of Davey. "As for ye, Ted Campbell..."

Neil unbuckled his belt and pulled it free of its loops. He wrapped one end round his hand, and advanced on Ted who was still lying dazed.

"Ah'll teach ye tae show me up."

He swung, and the buckle end hit Ted's back. Ted curled into a ball. His arms covered as much of his head as possible, as Neil straddled him and swung, again and again.

When Frank arrived back with Davey clutched to his chest, kicking and struggling, Neil stopped.

"Jist throw him down there. Ah'll get tae him when I'm through wi' Ted."

Frank let go of Davey and pushed him, but instead of falling, Davey stumbled forward and caught Neil behind the knees. Neil fell, and Davey shouted: "Run, Ted, run."

Neil and Davey grappled. Neil's hand, still wrapped in the belt, smashed twice into Davey's face and he slumped.

"Tie him, Ted. There's nae point in beatin' him till he's awake and can feel it. Right, sonny boy?"

As he spoke, Neil reached out to pat Ted's cheek and Ted drew back angrily, but he bent and rolled Davey over to tie his hands, and Neil laughed.

"There's some booze in the hut, Frank. This work gies me a thirst."

The two men sat and drank.

"Ted, light us a fire. A small one, mind. Nae smoke. We might as well have some comfort."

"Whit will we do with them?" Frank said.

"Angus says they're no expected back for about a week. So no one will miss them for three or four days. Ah'm goin' to kill them, yin at a time, slowly. Ah'm goin' tae enjoy this.

"Come on, Ted. Get that fire lit. Ah'm gettin' cold. There's plenty of space up on the moor. They won't be the first up there. They won't be the last."

Ted sat, head between his knees, arms wrapped round his legs, as the two men sat at the fire.

"Get us another bottle, Ted."

When Ted came back with the bottle, he got a back-hander from his father.

"Whit kept ye?"

The two men drank from the bottle twice each, and then slumped forward. Neil snored or snorted. After about five minutes, Ted approached us, knife in hand.

Davey, conscious again, looked apprehensively at Ted, but Ted rolled him over and cut his wrist bindings. Soon all three of us were free and rubbed circulation into painful hands and feet.

"Davey, collect all our stuff together," I said. "Thanks, Ted."

Ted made no reply; seated again, wrapped up in himself.

I looked in the hut and flashed my torch round.

"How long will they stay out?" Mike said, and when Ted made no reply, shook him.

"Maybe an hour, maybe longer," Ted shrugged. "Pa used tae use it on truck drivers. He slipped it into their coffee at truck stops, then Murray and Donald would steal the trucks."

"Everything of ours collected? No traces? Good," I said. "Now for them."

"Are ye goin' tae kill them?" Ted said, when I approached Neil, knife in hand.

"No. Just strip them."

I cut the clothing and pulled the clothes free.

"Right, Davey. That can there, pour it over them."

Davey looked at the label.

"Yellow marker dye, non-toxic, water proof," he read, and laughed.

"There's a Very Pistol there from the hut, put it in Old Man Campbell's hand and fire off a couple of flares. That'll bring someone."

We extinguished the fire and made a last check round.

"Let's go," Mike said.

We shouldered our packs, picked up our staffs and made for the edge of the clearing.

At the edge, Davey stopped and turned back.

"Coming, Ted?"

Thirty Six

Mike had Davey and Ted lead off down the fire break trail while he and I took turns of sweeping behind us. When we came across a small stream which intersected the trail, Mike said: "Follow the burn upstream."

About quarter of mile in from the trail, there was a small clearing. We stopped and Mike checked round.

"There are some small animal trails, Pete, nothing very big, and no sign of a human path. We'll stop here tonight. It's dusk anyway. There's no point in blundering around in the dark. Davey, a small fire. No smoke."

"Ah'll dae it," Ted said. "We'll need some sma' dry sticks."

We huddled close to the fire as dark closed round us, munching on sandwiches and some nuts, and drinking water from the burn.

There was a slightly embarrassed silence, then I said: "Thanks for cutting us loose, Ted."

"Would your dad really have killed us?" Davey said, and Ted shivered.

"Aye. Ah think so. He was aye beatin' on me or gettin' Donald to hurt me. The best times were when Donald was in jail and Pa was away from home."

We were silent. Ted looked from one to the other, suddenly apprehensive.

"Whit are ye three goin' tae dae wi' me?"

"We'll tie you up for now, we're tired. I know some great tortures," Davey said.

"Shut up, Davey," I snapped. "He's joking Ted, or trying to. You can go, or stay with us tonight. You're as free as we are."

Ted shivered again.

"Father McIntyre said ye could hae killed me the night Murray almost bought it. Davey could have bashed my brains in back there when he knocked me down – Peter stopped him. Davey dived at Pa when he was leatherin' me and gave me a chance tae run. Ah'll stay."

"Your dad was in jail and you were in care, Charlie McIntyre told us. What happened? How come you were with him?" Mike said.

"Pa's lawyer managed tae spring him twa, three days since. He served an order on the Remand Home tae release me tae Pa. 'A boy should be with his father,' he said."

Ted shifted uncomfortably. "We went tae Frank's place. Pa got drunk the first night and leathered me, for nothin', jist because he felt like it. Ah'll kill the big bastard some time. Ye'll see."

He rubbed his eyes.

"Anyone like a chocolate biscuit?" Davey said, and produced a packet of chocolate digestives.

"Mum'll kill you when we get back, Davey Lamont," Mike said.

We laughed, and helped ourselves to a biscuit.

Later, as we spread our bed rolls and sleeping bags, Davey said: "Where's Ted going to sleep? Pete, if we zip our two bags together, the three of us can sleep in them. Okay?"

Next morning in the dawn light, Mike looked at Davey's face, then turned him to the light.

"Hey, Pete. Come and look at this."

I whistled. The bruise where Neil Campbell's belt-wrapped fist had hit Davey was purple with black lines and partially closed the eye.

Gently, Davey explored his face with his hand.

"It doesn't feel too bad if you don't touch it. The lump behind my ear has gone down." Davey giggled. "You should see Ted's bum and his legs!"

"How did you see them?"

"Well. I had to go, you know, and Ted was just pulling his pants up. So I sort of saw him."

"Ted, pull up your shirt and let's see your back," Mike said.

"Why should Ah? Who are ye tae tell me what tae dae?"

"Come on, Ted. In the wood, Mike's boss," Davey said.

"We only want to see your bruises. To see if we have to go back for a doctor," I said.

Ted peeled off his shirt and we looked.

"Wow! Drop them, Ted."

Ted hesitated.

"Come on, or Pete and I will hold you for Davey."

Reluctantly, Ted dropped his pants and his shorts. His back, buttocks and thighs were a mass of bruises, old and new.

"You're not bleeding anyplace. Do you feel all right?"

"No' any worse than usual," Ted said, and started to dress.

"What say, Mike?"

"He's all right, I think, Pete. Let's stay out."

"What about Ted?" Davey said.

"Do you want to stay with us?" I said, and looked at the others. "Can he?"

Mike and Davey nodded.

"Okay. Ah'll stick around for a while, but no funny stuff."

He looked at us in utter amazement as the three of us clung to each other, helpless with laughter.

"We're four in the wood again," Davey gasped, and put out a hand to Ted to draw him into the group.

 # Thirty Seven

We spent five days in the wood and on the heath, eating what we could catch there and in the loch. Our oatmeal ran out on the fourth day; the biscuits, much to Davey's disgust, on the second.

When we made our way back to catch the ferry to the island, Ted said: "Whit about me? Ah'm no goin' back with Pa and Ah dinnae want tae gae back tae the Remand Centre."

"Your dad won't be on the loose to go back to, not if the police looked in the shed," I said. "Come back to the island with us. Charlie and Mr Buchanan should be able to set something up."

We boarded the ferry without incident, although I thought the First Officer looked rather oddly at us.

When the ferry docked at the island, Mike said: "Oh, Oh! We've got a reception committee. Look!"

Mr Buchanan, Charlie, Alf, and Uncle Alex were waiting on the quay, and a short distance off, Inspector Cameron and a constable. Shortly before the ferry actually tied up, I saw a black Rolls Royce pull onto the pier and slide into the Harbour Master's parking slot.

We filed down the gangplank, me in the lead and Mike at the rear. Mr Buchanan and his group reached us first, but only marginally before the police.

"Ted Campbell, you will come with me, please," Inspector Cameron said. "Constable, take him."

The Duke arrived breathless.

"Let's go into the Harbour Master's Office, please."

It was a command rather than a request, and we all trooped off the quay.

"We'll use your office if you don't mind," the Duke informed the Harbour Master as we swept in.

"Cameron, you start."

"The mainland police picked up Neil Campbell, blind drunk, unconscious, naked and covered in yellow dye beside a disused fire hut. It was full of stolen goods. His prints were everywhere. He had a Very Pistol in his hand. It had been fired twice. When he came round, he babbled on about three boys who had ambushed him and his equally drunk and naked friend, and had abducted his son. He's back in jail. Ted is to go back into Care."

Ted looked resigned.

I had been whispering furiously to Alf and the Duke, and when Inspector Cameron stopped, the Duke held up his hand.

"Inspector Cameron. This is certainly Ted Campbell. Are there any charges current or pending against him?"

"No, Your Grace. His father is in prison and likely to be there for some time now. Murray and Donald are also in jail and there are no other relatives we know of."

"Fine. I would like him taken to the local hospital, where my solicitor will meet us. Can you arrange for Dr. Wilkins and an official photographer – oh, that's you, Buchanan, isn't it – to be there too. There will be other charges against Campbell, I think. After that, I expect Ted Campbell to be released into the custody of Alf Turner. I will stand surety for him."

Mike and I both spoke quietly to Ted and Davey slapped his back as he went off with the police and the Duke.

"I'll collect my equipment and meet you there," Mr Buchanan said.

Alf hugged Davey and grinned at Mike and me.

"You had us worried. We only heard after you'd gone to ground that Neil Campbell was on the loose again."

Mr Buchanan scowled at him.

"When word came out about the yellow birds, we assumed you were all right. Well, at least no one got killed this time out," Mr Buchanan grumbled. "I have to say it was a limited success and that you did well. I'll see you later. I'd better move and get to the hospital."

"Uncle Alex, I'm sorry we worried you."

Alex Lamont smiled.

"They let me in on it, but Grandpa and Aunt Jean don't know, neither do the Calders. You were just camping as planned. I don't know what we're to tell Jean about Davey's face."

That evening, we met in the gym for a debrief session – a post mortem, the Duke called it.

I described the events of the five days.

"So the only one who actually used his training in fighting was Davey? Fighting with Ted, I mean," Mr Buchanan said. "How do you explain that? Not a particularly brilliant performance, was it?"

"We weren't expecting anything, Dad. We were relaxed," Mike said. "On holiday."

"When you have enemies who might be looking for you, you can't afford that kind of holiday."

"Lighten up, Murdoch. Don't ride the boys," Charlie said. "If we'd known Campbell was out we wouldn't have let them go on the trip, not unescorted anyway."

Both Gordon McLeod and Alf scowled and started to speak. It was obviously a sore point with the group.

I held my hand up.

"Stop it. All of you. We're fine. We had a swell time. We're here. If our info network broke down, then fix it so it doesn't happen again. Don't keep chewing over the past. That's right, isn't it, Major? Learn and move on. Don't let our feelings cloud our judgement."

"Pete's right," Alf said.

"Yes, suits you. It lets you and Gordon off the hook," Mr Buchanan snapped.

My right hand chopped down and the Duke laughed.

"That will do!" I said. "Do you two know what happened?"

Alf and Gordon nodded.

"You can fix it?"

"Yes, Pete," Alf said.

"Then do so. Right, the subject is closed. Now, why wasn't Davey able to use any of the tricks to escape Frank?"

"Aw, Pete. Don't start on me. It's finished, you said."

"No, Davey. I'm not blaming you, but we have to know. Why couldn't you?"

"I was scared, I suppose. After I knocked Ted Campbell down, I ran. I didn't think of anything except to get the hell out there. I tripped over a root and Frank jumped on me. He must weigh a ton at least. I could hardly breathe when he lifted me. He just wrapped his arms right round me and squeezed. I kicked, but I couldn't get my knees far enough up to hit anyplace that mattered."

"Suggestions?" I said. "Alf, Charlie?"

"How high was he holding you?" Alf said.

"I don't know. I'd my back to him trying to breathe."

"Davey's shoulders were level with Frank's," Mike said.

"You could have snapped your head back, as hard and as fast as you could. With luck you might have broken his nose or at least loosened some teeth. Right, Charlie?"

Nodding, Charlie said: "Unless you are permanently on guard, you can always be knocked out in a surprise attack. We've been concentrating on fighting when you expect to fight. We haven't done anything on escapes, or how to deal with the sort of situation Davey faced."

"Right," I said, "that about wraps it up. We all know what we have to learn and do now?"

The adults nodded, and Davey and Mike looked warily at me. They had not seen me take over The Group before.

"What about Ted? What's the word on him?"

"He's still at the hospital, Pete," Alf said. "Wilkins examined every inch of him and Murdoch photographed him. Ted wasn't exactly pleased. Murdoch said he'd send the photos to Playgirl. Wilkins had him x-rayed too. Statements have been taken. Neil Campbell will have some extra charges to face. I'd like some time alone with Neil Campbell in a dark alley."

"When will Ted be out and what then?"

"Wilkins is holding him till tomorrow. Some lab tests he wants done. Then Ted'll come home with me. I've got a spare room. Gerry's mouthpiece is setting it up. I'm going to foster him. We'll be fine. We have a lot in common. Well, I'm going back to the hospital now. 'Night all."

The group broke up and Mike said: "Can we all come up for some cocoa, Dad?"

Mike and Davey ran on ahead, and as we walked Mr Buchanan put a hand on my shoulder.

"Well done, Pete. Not the camping trip; that was a disaster – the beginning anyway – but tonight. We were squabbling because we thought we had let you down. You got us back on track. Whether you like it or not, you're almost ready."

"Did Mrs Buchanan miss a packet of biscuits?"

"Lord! I forgot all about them. She'll chew Davey up and spit out the bits. Quick, let's catch up on them."

He slapped me on the rump and we ran up the road.

Thirty Eight

Later that night, I waited till Davey was asleep and the house was quiet, then slipped down to talk to Grandpa.

To my surprise and alarm, Grandpa was not in the lounge. His chair at the window was empty. In a panic, I remembered Aunt Jean had said earlier that Grandpa was unwell.

"Is that you, Peter?"

Grandpa's voice came from his room.

Relieved, I went in to find Grandpa in bed. He leaned back against a large pile of pillows.

"Are you all right, Grandpa?"

"Yes, I'm fine. I've had turns like this before. I'll be A1 in the morning. Come on in and sit with me a while."

I told Grandpa about my evening: that in our usual walk Davey had gone off arm in arm with Joan leaving me to walk by myself.

"Are you upset or annoyed with Davey or Joan?"

I thought for a while before I said slowly: "No. Davey has grown up recently and he and Joan see a lot of each other at the stables and the school. My head's been full of other junk lately. If it's anyone's fault, it's mine."

"You've grown up a lot too. More than some ever do."

We sat quiet for a long time.

"You're very like your grandfather, Peter. Davey's other grandfather, Jean's father. He used to write poetry. I've seen some of your essays. They're good. Have you written any poems?"

"Just one," I said. "It's a poem about time. We were reading about theories of the universe; Sir James Jeans, the Astronomer, I think. Something about the universe being either bounded but infinite, or unbounded but finite. It was neat. It clicked with something both Keith and Mr Buchanan said."

In a dreamy voice I said: "I called it *The Ocean*.

"The ocean of time is finite, boundless is its reach
An endless chaos of tumbling waters deep
Currents there are beneath the waves,
patterns to the storms.
He who knows may navigate the endless, trackless deeps
The jetsam of the gods, man drifts
An aimless pointless journey?
Which will be dashed on rock?
Which will reach safe haven?
Is one fate good another bad?
How does it serve the Great Design, if such there be?
A nobler span than man's can grasp the ocean's whole
A viewpoint from far off can see the Grand Design
Currents there are beneath the waves,
patterns to the storms.
He who knows may navigate the endless, trackless deeps."

"Peter, you're going back. Aren't you?"

"Perhaps, Grandpa. I don't want to leave you."

"Have you decided who goes with you?"

"Mr Buchanan asked that too. There's plenty of time."

"No, Peter. There are only certain windows or doorways available. If you don't go back at the next Hunt, you may have missed it for years. By then, it only will be a boyish dream. Don't worry about me. I love you and Davey, but you know, I sometimes didn't make a move so as not to leave friends, only to find the friends moved away and left me behind. This year has been great. I thought I had lost Davey for ever, but he came back, with you for a bonus. I have enjoyed having both of you."

I squeezed Grandpa's hand.

"Without you and Mr Buchanan, I wouldn't have made it here."

"I'm going to sleep for a while, Peter."

"Can I lie beside you on the bed? I won't disturb you."

I wakened with a start, then remembered where I was. A cover had been thrown over me. What was the croaking, rattling noise I'd heard? Well, it hadn't disturbed Grandpa.

A little later I wakened again.

Grandpa's hand was cold and heavy on my back.

 **Thirty Nine**

I went through the funeral in a daze. I found the Presbyterian service cold and very short and, for me, not very comforting. It was only at the lunch after I realised what a crowd had attended.

The expected locals were there; Uncle Alex was a respected and well known businessman on the island, a fair number of men and women of about Grandpa's age, and a surprising number of men who ranged in age from about Mr Buchanan's age to about fifteen years older. At the lunch I noticed two in particular whom Mr Buchanan, Charlie and the Duke addressed as 'Sir'.

In the typical post-funeral release everyone talked about events from Grandpa's life. Davey grabbed my elbow.

"Did you see all those geezers after the church service? The funeral director practically had a fit. They insisted on walking behind the hearse. Grandpa would have laughed. They argued about march order. Something about current rank, or rank at retiral, or date of training under Grandpa. Alf soon sorted them out. It's a good job it was only a short way to the cemetery."

The house felt empty, deserted, despite the presence of Davey's brothers and sister and their families over on the island for the funeral, then suddenly there were too many people. I excused myself to Aunt Jean and left the house. I sat on the pier where we sat when Davey had his encounter with the dogs, and laughed at the memory. A hand fell on my shoulder, and I jumped.

"That's it, Pete," Alf said. "Remember the good times. That's what the others are doing up at the hotel."

"Why aren't you with them?"

"Oh, all that brass don't want a non-com drinking with them. The RSM trained some very successful men, you know. Anyway, my place is with you now."

"Alf, you know I'm Catholic?"

"So am I, Pete." Alf laughed. "I should be insulted. You should see your face. I'm what Charlie calls a lapsed Catholic, a strayed sheep."

"Do you think Charlie would say a Requiem Mass for Grandpa?"

"He will if you want him to, or I'll break his head."

"Do you think Grandpa would mind?"

Alf laughed. "If half the stories the brass are telling about him are even half true, he needs all the help he can get to push through the Pearly Gates. He was no saint you know, Pete. Just a man like all of us. Besides, would Grandpa object to anything that would give you some comfort?"

I turned and leant my head against Alf. Alf simply held my head into him and patted my shoulders gently.

"Cry now; later, people won't have the patience for it."

We stayed, motionless on the deserted, rain and windswept pier for ages before Alf said: "About cried out? Here, wipe your eyes. Let's walk out to the tearoom at the point for a cuppa. Okay. You can have coffee if you'd rather."

I laughed and rose, and we walked off arm in arm.

The Requiem Mass was well attended. To everyone's surprise Uncle Alex not only made no objection, but even announced his intention of attending.

Davey said, "Don't worry, Pete. I'll sit with Dad and make sure he knows when to bob up and down."

Aunt Ina had sniffed and said to Charlie: "I don't know what you're thinking of, Father McIntyre. He wasn't Catholic, and not even a blood relative of Peter's."

Charlie scowled ferociously. "As Our Lord said, Mrs Calder, 'In My Father's House there are many mansions.' I hope my lack of charity will be forgiven when I say I hope we don't end in the same one."

Forty

About two weeks after the funeral, I sat in Grandpa's chair and gazed, unseeing, out at the dark sea.

"Who's there?" I said, when I heard a board creak.

"It's you, Peter. Lord, you gave me a fright," Aunt Jean said. "I heard a noise down here. Even when you spoke you sounded like Grandpa."

She sat on the arm of the chair and put an arm round me, and I leaned back against her. "Miss him, Pete? We all do. We can't bring him back. It's all part of life. Grandpa had a good life. He enjoyed himself."

"I'm all right. I was only sitting thinking."

"I'll make some cocoa, Peter."

We sat facing each other and sipped the cocoa.

"Want to talk? Have you been sitting up like this much?"

"Really, I'm fine. Davey's more upset about Grandpa than me. Grandpa's somewhen else, that's all."

"Is everything still all right between you and Davey? I don't want to interfere, or be nosey, but I do love you both and don't want anything to come between you."

"Don't beat around the bush, Aunt Jean. You're talking about Joan?"

"Yes. For a while you were a crowd, but lately Davey's real smitten with Joan. He talks about her endlessly. Alex and I thought

201

you and Joan were taken with each other and we worried that …
Well, that you might be jealous of each other and fight."

I grinned. "When we were just a crowd, Davey thought the
girls were in the way, and yes, I suppose I liked Joan best. There
are no hard feelings. Davey's not even aware he 'queered my
pitch' as Grandpa put it. It's up to Joan anyway."

Jean reached over and patted my knee. "You can be rivals
without fighting, but it is good you feel that way. Who is
Margaret?"

I choked on my cocoa. "How did you hear of her?"

"I spoke to Davey about him and Joan, and he said: 'After all
he has Margaret'."

"She's a girl I met a while ago. Davey had no right to tell you."

"Sorry, Peter. I didn't mean to start anything. What is the
Duke's stake in all this? Do you know what the town gossip is?"

"I didn't know people were gossiping."

"Some are. It hasn't gone unnoticed that the Duke is still here
and for the first time anyone can remember, island children, well,
young people, are visiting the estate regularly.

"Some are saying only the Duke could have managed to have
you disappear then reappear. He controlled the guards at both
closed days."

"Why would he want to do that? What would he want with five
boys for a year?"

"The gossip doesn't say, Peter. Two of you didn't come back,
remember?"

"The truth is even more difficult to believe," I said, after a long
thoughtful pause.

"You do remember, don't you? Grandpa knew, didn't he, and
Helen Buchanan?"

"Yes, Aunt Jean, we all do."

After another silence, I told Jean the story, omitting only the
Duke's – my Duke's – presence in my head.

"You're right, Peter. It is pretty unbelievable. Why all the training? What is that all in aid of?" Aunt Jean stopped, a horrified expression on her face. "You're going back."

We studied each other.

"You're not taking my Davey back, Peter Macdonald. You're not."

I slid to the floor and knelt beside Aunt Jean.

"I don't know. Sometimes I do want to go back, sometimes I want to stay here. Mr Buchanan thinks I might not have a choice. That's what the training is about."

"Why would you want to go back?"

"It's very difficult to explain. I feel I'm needed there. All the Duke's records, so Davey and Mike say, show us being there. I'm afraid too. If we don't go back, will we simply blink out of existence then and now? Something eliminated when a time warp or loop gets corrected? Which is our time anyway, then or now?"

"Peter, your family is here and your friends."

"I've got family there too, and friends. Margaret, the girl Davey mentioned – remember? – the girl I met in the past, is there. Aunt Jean, if it's my choice, I won't take Davey back if he doesn't want to go."

"I'm sorry I snapped, Peter. I know none of this is your fault, but I don't want to lose Davey or you again." She blew her nose and wiped her eyes. "Off to bed with you, Peter. There's still school tomorrow and I've got a lot to think about."

 **Forty One**

One lunch, Mike was at Uncle John's workshop, Davey was at the stables, as he was most days now school was out, and I went home.

"Want a sandwich, Peter? I'm too busy to stop for much else," Aunt Jean said.

"I'll make them." I worked in silence and watched Aunt Jean fuss with the laundry. "Want me to make some tea?"

Aunt Jean nodded, turned away, then turned back to me and shook me. "What are you up to now, Peter?"

"Nothing. Honest."

She hugged me hard. "I don't want to lose you two again. Helen Buchanan and I talked about it. She says we'll lose all three of you in a few years anyway. That's different. Oh, Peter. Don't take Davey."

"Sometimes I think this is how soldiers home on leave must have felt. A home and people they love in one place and other people who depend on them, and a duty, someplace else. Sometimes someone they love there too."

"In your case Keith, the boy who didn't come back with you three, and Margaret?"

"Yes, and others. We, well, I anyway, swore to defend the infant duke and his succession."

After a short silence, I said: "We didn't have a choice last Hunt. We were in the wood and it happened."

"You don't need to be in the wood this year on Hunt Day, Peter, any of you."

"I'm all mixed up. I don't know exactly what I want. I promise I'll try not to influence Davey."

"I suppose I'll have to be content with that. Peter, you're so like my father. He was a stubborn, determined man. Once he'd decided where his duty lay, nothing and no one could deflect him."

 **Forty Two**

"Whit are we doin' here anyway? There's lots better places tae camp. Less spooky places." Ted peered round him in the flickering light of the fire.

"Well, Pete?" Alf said.

"I want to be in the chapel, but I'm not suicidal. I want you to know where I am, and be ready to pull me back."

I had persuaded the others to camp overnight at the monastery ruins.

"Pete, we're so close to Hunt time, four weeks," Mike said. "Shouldn't we wait till then and see what happens?"

"You nearly died here last time," Alf said. "I don't like this."

"That's why I wanted everyone here. You can take turns standing guard."

"Thanks a lot. Just what I wanted to do. Sit up all night watching you."

"Shut up, Davey. I need to know what's happening, if I can. You and Mike need information to make up your minds too. So take your turn with less lip."

"I'm joking, Pete. Don't get all stuffy."

"You and Mike bed down first. Alf and Ted will wake you when it's your turn, if you're needed."

I turned and walked off to where the centre of the chapel should be. Alf signalled to Ted and they followed me.

"Kneel with me," I said.

When the air on my face changed from the fresh outside air to the incense laden air of the chapel, I opened my eyes. There was no light, except the faint red glow of the vigil light before the reserved host, and I peered through the gloom. The chapel was empty. I thought hard.

Please come, Keith. I can't wander through the monastery searching for you. I haven't a clue where you sleep now. If I wander, I'll create a riot with everyone seeing ghosts.

My knees were sore and stiff before I heard the soft slip-slop of sandals and the thump of Keith's staff. Relieved, I climbed to my feet, as flickering shadows slithered into the chapel.

"It is Pete, Bernard. I know it is. It must be," came Keith's voice.

Bernard's deep rumble followed: "Quietly, Master Keith, quietly. Let's not have the whole house in an uproar. With the Lord Abbot away, the master of novices might have you whipped."

They advanced into the chapel and I rushed to them.

Greetings over, Bernard said: "Who have you with you, Master Peter?"

He pointed and I turned. Two figures knelt, rigid, blank faced in the flickering light. As the three of us looked, one figure then the other stirred.

"It's the man-servant we saw last time and a youth," Bernard said, advancing on them.

Alf looked round him pale-faced, then spotted me.

"Lord, Pete. What have you got us into now?"

At Alf's voice, Ted lowered his hands from his eyes where they had flown after a first quick look. He crossed himself.

"It's a dream. It's got to be a dream. Oh God, make it a dream. I'm at home in bed."

He shrieked as Bernard touched him, and I dashed to his side. Keith hobbled up as fast as he could.

"Shh, Ted, shh. You'll waken everyone."

"Oh, I'm still here. They're still here."

Keith knelt beside him and put out a hand.

"Campbell! It's Ted Campbell," Keith said. "Well I'll be damned."

Bernard crossed himself, and half drew his dagger.

"It's aw richt, Bernard. It's a thing we say, will say, used to say? Ah'm aw confused. It means Ah'm very surprised."

"Keith Stone? Where are we? Is this hell?"

"Stop babbling, Ted," Keith said. "By Aw the Saints, Ah oft dreamed o' haein' ye frichtened o' me, and noo ye are, Ah cannae dae awthing. Naw, this isnae hell. Here, get up."

I helped Keith to his feet, then Ted.

"Do you two know each other?"

Ted nodded, shivered, and cowered against me. Keith laughed.

"We lived in the same part of toon. Didn't we, Ted? Ah wis ane o' Ted's regulars. He used tae try oot new torments on me. Between him, Pa an' ma brithers it wis hell."

Ted licked dry lips with a parched tongue.

"Ah'm no like that any more," he croaked. "Oh God, please make it a nightmare."

"Ted's with us now," I said. "He's Okay. I'll explain it all sometime, Keith, but not now. We have to talk. Come on, Ted, get a grip on yourself. Keith and Bernard are friends."

Ted still clung to my arm.

"Alf, Bernard, take him. Talk him down."

Bernard and Alf had watched. Alf now looked at Bernard.

"I've looked after him as best I could," he said, and rubbed his ear, "but it's a little like holding an eel or a greased pig."

Bernard laughed and bowed. "Bernard, servant to Master Keith and to the Lord of Möbius."

"Alf, Alfred really. Alf to my friends. Chief Factotum to His Lordship here."

"Come on you two. See if you can talk some sense into Ted. He's frightened."

Keith and I withdrew to a wall niche and talked quietly.

"Quick, Pete. Something's happened to Ted."

When I reached the bench, Alf had Ted stretched out flat. Even in the dim light, his face looked ashen. His skin was cold and clammy to the touch, his breathing gasping, irregular.

"What is it, Alf? What's wrong with him?"

"How should I know? He suddenly started gasping for air, then keeled over."

"Quick. Put Ted where he was, more or less, when you came through. Now whereabouts would Mike and Davey be sleeping?"

I thought hard, trying to visualise where we were in relation to the ruins and the ground of that time.

"About here?" I said.

Alf nodded. "I think so."

I knelt, and closed my eyes.

"Aw Pete, get off. You're too heavy."

I heard the voice in the distance. There was something I had to do. If things would only stop going round, I could think.

"Mike. Wake up, Mike. You great lout. Help me with Pete," Davey said.

I struggled to a sitting position, and said: "No. I'll be okay now. See to Alf and Ted."

We turned to face the hollow in the ruins where the chapel had been. Two figures lay there.

"Quick, pull Alf up. He'll come round soon the way I did. Let me see Ted."

Alf shook his head. "I think I'll look for another job, if you don't mind, Pete, one with less travelling maybe?"

"Get out of my way, all of you," Mike said.

He opened Ted's anorak and ripped open the shirt. Ear pressed hard to Ted's bare chest, he listened for a moment before he knelt beside Ted, and placed a hand, palm down on his chest.

"I hope I remember how to do this right."

One hand on top of the other, Mike pushed down with all his weight and relaxed quickly, then repeated the process before placing his ear on the bare chest again.

Next time he found his spot and brought his clenched fist down hard, and listened again. Grasping Ted's nose, Mike pulled the head back and opened the mouth. He fished around the mouth for the tongue, before blowing hard into Ted's mouth, squinting to watch the chest.

"Here, I can do that," Alf said, but Mike sat back and grinned as Ted's chest rose and fell on its own.

We carried Ted to the jeep, and sped into town.

At the hospital, we waited anxiously, in silence, as the duty intern examined Ted. When he appeared we crowded round him.

"How is he?" Alf said.

"He's resting quite comfortably now, but I've sent for Dr Wilkins. He's on call for emergency tonight. I'm a bit puzzled. Ah, here's Dr Wilkins now."

Dr Wilkins swept past us with no more than a curt nod. He was a long time, I thought, worried, but when he finally emerged he smiled at us, a little grimly perhaps, but still a smile.

"Young Campbell will be fine. He's asleep now. You can see him in the morning."

Dr Wilkins drew Alf aside, but not so far that I couldn't hear.

"What was the problem?" Alf said.

"He wasn't well looked after as a child. Neglected in fact. Suffered a lot of abuse, I'd say. Had rheumatic fever and not properly cared for, or supervised after. Some residual valve weakness, I suspect."

"Why didn't you tell me this when I said I'd look after him?"

"There was nothing to tell you then. I had the history, but nothing showed up during examination. A query, perhaps, at best. If I frightened everyone in this part of the country about their valves, about a third of my patients would be afraid to exert themselves. Such minor valve defects are endemic here. The soft water – lack of dissolved minerals – some speculate. Anyway, I wouldn't have restricted his activities then." Dr Wilkins paused. "I suppose I should have considered he was going to be associated with Genghis Khan here and his horde."

"That's not fair, Doctor. Peter's a good lad. So are the others. Have you any complaints about the girls' chumming around with them?"

"No, I haven't, true, but Ted's a Campbell. I imagine Donald and his father have different views of these boys – Murray too. There is something very odd about them. Remember I was the first to see them after they were found in the wood. Have you seen them naked?"

Alf nodded.

"Waddell, the psychologist, couldn't get past the block Peter set up. He was sure the boy was hiding something, and preventing the others from telling too. If you ask him now, he looks blank, then smiles, 'Oh, that kid? A very normal boy in every way, but a bit of a nonentity.' I ask you, Mr Turner, would you describe Peter as a nonentity?"

With a grin, Alf said: "No, I wouldn't, but then I'm prejudiced, I suppose."

"I'm going to keep young Campbell in till tomorrow. What you describe sounds like a mild heart attack. He has a bruise on his chest. If your story's correct, Michael may have saved his life – if the blow, or a beating, wasn't the cause of the event in the first place."

As Alf started to protest, Dr Wilkins held up his hand.

"Ted tells a confused story about ghosts at the monastery. Some boy he used to bully, and an ugly man with one ear. Too many of Peter's sausages? And some nasty campfire tales? If that's the case, Ted's valve condition is more advanced than I thought. Have it checked out. In the meantime, no silly overexertion, but don't coddle him – no time travel, of course!"

Dr Wilkins laughed and left.

I sent the others back to Alf's place, instructing Alf to let the Lamonts and the Buchanans know what had happened.

 **Forty Three**

Early in the morning Ted stirred, and I wondered if I should call the nurse, but Ted was quite relaxed.

Squeezing Ted's hand I said: "Hi, Ted. It's me, Pete. We're in the hospital on the island. You're fine."

"Whit happened? It wis a dream, wisn't it?"

Quietly, I told Ted the story of the missing year.

"Keith Stone got left behind? For real?"

"Yes, Ted. He was tortured and couldn't travel back with us."

Ted began to tremble violently and I sat on the bed to hold him.

"I've been back, sort of, twice now. I needed someone to pull me back here first time. Honest, I didn't know that you and Alf would go through with me. I suppose your knowing Keith and me did it. Keith and Bernard wouldn't have hurt you. Like you, Keith's changed, and anyway you were with me."

"Ah wisnae frightened o' them. Honest, Ah don't think I was, but suddenly Ah jist couldnae breathe. It was as if someone sat on my chest and pressed really hard. Then everythin' went black."

Dr Wilkins was in before eleven and was quite satisfied with Ted's condition.

"You can go as soon as either Mr Turner or one of the Lamonts comes to sign you out. Have them call me."

Alf came to pick us up and drove us first to the gym, where Mr Buchanan had asked for a meeting.

213

Except for Gordon McLeod, who was off-island on holiday, all The Group was there.

"Before anyone tries to chew Alf out about allowing last night," I glared at Mr Buchanan, "Alf couldn't have stopped me. I'd decided I needed the information. If Alf hadn't agreed I'd have tried on my own."

"What about Ted?" Charlie said. "Who asked him?"

"Yes, I've already said I'm sorry about that. I didn't expect either Alf or Ted to come through with me. Charlie, what do you think, did I really go or did only my mind travel?"

"That other time at the monastery," Alf said, "I couldn't swear to it, but I thought when Mike and I got there, the ruins were deserted. That could simply have been the light, but I did see Keith and Bernard One Ear."

"Last night was real then," Ted said. "Ah really did see Keith Stone. He touched me."

"Were our bodies there, or just our minds?"

"You must have moved your body, Pete," Davey said. "I was having a swell dream, till you fell on me. Shrinks say that kind of event could warp my development."

"Shut up, Davey," Mike said. "Nothing could warp you any further."

"I was dreaming about Joan. Then suddenly it was Pete I was hugging. What a letdown."

"What's your point, Pete?" Charlie said.

"Well, it's almost Hunt time. I think there is a time window – the Day of the Hunt – when it is possible to go through, body and mind, and stay without harm. The other times I'm not sure. What I wonder is, if there is a place window too? Only one place that is completely safe, or is the monastery an alternate?"

"Why, Pete?"

"Joan says her father is going to have the wood locked up so tight for those twenty four hours that not even a flea could get through. Nobody's going missing in his manor this August."

"When did she tell you that?" Davey said.

"Pete and Joan actually talk to each other, lover boy," Mike said and ducked.

"Stow it, you two," Alf said. "Have you made up your mind?"

"Yes. I'm going back, if I can. The neighbouring lords want to put in someone else to rule in place of the infant duke, someone of their choosing."

"Dad, I've got to go back," Mike said. "Robert and our friends need us."

"To say nothing of Robert's daughters." Davey grinned.

"What if we don't go back?" I said. "Does our time, as such, cease or change drastically? Davey and I, at least, are descended from the Peter of that time."

"Let's leave it," Mike said. "It's a paradox we're not going to resolve. Pete and I are going back, if we can. We have a more immediate practical problem. Can Inspector Cameron seal up the wood? If he does, can Pete and I get back via the monastery?"

"What about me?" Davey said. Mike looked hard at him.

"Well, what about you? Are you coming or not?"

 **Forty Four**

When the Duke heard Ted had been waitlisted for a full examination at the regional hospital, he was furious and within twenty four hours had arranged an immediate appointment with a heart specialist.

Ted was sent off-island to the doctor and three days later the Duke sent for me.

"I've got the medical report. What were your plans for Ted?"

"That was really up to him, Uncle Gerry, but I thought he might come with us."

The Duke shook his head.

"The report says he has exercise induced arrhythmia, related to a valve condition that could be congenital or a result of rheumatic fever as a child."

"What does it mean to us or to him?"

"I'll jump to the summary and recommendations: 'No restrictions on normal activities. He should be seen regularly by a doctor to check for possible valve deterioration. I would not pass him as fit for active military service'."

"So Ted has to stay here in this time?" I finally said, after a silence. "You will look after the Lamonts and the Calders, and see Ted is cared for?"

"I will, My Lord."

I scowled at the Duke, but his face was serious, solemn even, and the tone was not sarcastic.

"As my line and honour depend on it, Lord Peter."

The remaining days before the Hunt anniversary passed like a slow motion dream.

Uncle John and Aunt Ina were oblivious to the seething excitement and anticipation. Uncle Alex was equally unaware. Aunt Jean was fine most of the time, but I found her red-eyed and upset on two occasions when I was home for lunch and the others were out.

One night, she joined me in the lounge while I sat in Grandpa's chair. I told her Inspector Cameron was going to post guards on the wood, and she looked relieved. Next day, I saw her coming out of the police station smiling and serene.

Joan and Irene were sent off-island on a visit to a relative of Irene's, much to Davey's annoyance.

With Mr and Mrs Buchanan everything went on much as before. Mr Buchanan now treated me with a curious mixture of familiarity and respect, in fact, I thought, rather the way Alf treated Mr Buchanan. Mrs Buchanan continued to treat us all, Mr Buchanan included, as small boys in need of a hug and a smack in equal proportions. She did, however, relent a little in her war with Davey over the biscuit tin.

My head was in a constant state of turmoil. Gerald had been true to his word and had not attempted to interfere or to influence me. Now the Hunt anniversary was so close, however, and since I had decided, there was a constant feeling of slightly apprehensive anticipation. It was difficult, I found, to separate my own feelings from Gerald's. There was no certainty we could go back. Had the Duke's death broken the link? If we couldn't get into the wood, or if I couldn't, would anything happen? What if I changed my mind?

"Peter! The link is not broken! I am here with you. I will always be with you. I have been silent as I promised not to influence you, but I am here.

"Don't even think of such a possibility, my son. Think of Keith, your friends there, my son of the flesh, the infant duke whom you swore to support, Margaret. Yes, Peter, think of Margaret. Would you have her betrothed to another? Think of Margaret."

Hunt Day dawned at last, and we met early in the morning on the beach where Colin's cairn had been those centuries ago. Our rock was now in a tiny cramped park surrounded by houses. Listlessly, we drifted to the wood, to the gate where two years ago Davey and I had first been told the wood was closed.

The wood was already sealed, with gamekeepers sweeping the entire area to make sure it was clear.

"It's only just gone ten," Davey said.

"The Hunt doesn't start till noon. I'm going to church," I said.

The others, a little surprised agreed: "Yes, we should, like the Hunt Mass last year."

"Which Mass did the Abbot say?" Charlie asked, when I explained why we were there.

"Aren't they all the same?" Davey said.

I thought.

"He said the Mass for the Dead."

"It is a little irregular, but I will say Mass for you, Pete, for all of you, if you wish."

Charlie had barely finished when Father McGuire strode in.

"What is the meaning of this, Father? A Latin Mass? These boys," he gestured at Davey and Mike, "are not even Catholic, and that was the old Latin Mass for the Dead."

"Yes, Father," Charlie said. "I will explain later. Excuse us."

We were suddenly all boisterous and, Charlie included, we ran along the beach toward the town, whooping. Breathless, we stopped at the pier.

"Ice cream?" Charlie said.

"Double nougats?" Davey said hopefully, and I, laughing almost hysterically, gasped out: " 'Ware reiving dogs, Davey, as Grandpa called the mutts who stole your ice cream, and watch out for flying cows."

 **Forty Five**

Just after noon Davey and I arrived home for lunch. We had barely stepped in the door before Aunt Jean gave Davey a note and some wrapped sandwiches.

"Take these to your dad, Davey, and pick up that stuff from the grocer's on your way back."

Davey looked at the list and sighed. "Oh, okay. Coming, Pete?"

"No," Aunt Jean said. "I want to talk to Peter."

With Davey gone, Aunt Jean sat with me in the living room.

"Ina Calder phoned me …"

Wow! The age of miracles wasn't past. Aunt Ina hadn't spoken to Aunt Jean since the disastrous meeting when Mom and Dad were here for Christmas.

"Peter! Are you listening to me? Ina says her priest told her that curate – Father Charlie – said a Mass for the three of you. An old Latin Mass, the Mass for the Dead. She said it was very strange with Davey not being Catholic. She thought I should know. What does it mean?"

"We thought it was right – like a sort of remembrance service …" I said.

"You've made up your mind to go back haven't you?" Aunt Jean dabbed at her eyes, then to my surprise smiled. "It won't work, you know. Right after Ina Calder's call I phoned Inspector

Cameron to tell him about the Mass. He says there is no way anyone can get into the wood between noon today and noon tomorrow. There are even some extra men coming from off-island to help patrol the perimeter."

Then maybe it'll have to be the monastery after all – the alternate site?

"I know that look, Peter Macdonald. You have made up your mind. You're just like my father, your grandfather, stubborn and pig-headed, but I tell you it won't work. Inspector Cameron has put guards on the old monastery ruins as well. If any of you try to get into either place he promised he'll arrest you and hold you in the cells until after noon tomorrow. I tried to persuade him to lock you all up now, but he said he couldn't until you actually tried something."

I felt really sorry about Aunt Jean's concern, but at the same time relieved. I hadn't needed to lie to her about my intentions. She was sure the unwitting tip-off from Aunt Ina and her calls to Inspector Cameron would make it impossible for us to be in the wood or at the monastery at the correct times. She looked happier now than she'd been for the past few weeks.

"As soon as Davey gets back we'll have lunch. I've got those little sausage rolls he likes and an apple tart."

"What did Mum want?" Davey said as we washed our hands before lunch. "She's all happy and smiling. Dad was sure surprised at the extra sandwiches. He'd taken his with him as usual when he went out this morning."

I filled Davey in on our conversation and he looked very thoughtful. "Is that it, then?"

"Your mom thinks she's got me cornered. I'll have to talk to Mr Buchanan."

That afternoon I told Mr Buchanan about Aunt Jean's report and told him that regardless, I, anyway, would be at our gym at 11.00pm and that he should let the others know I was determined to try, despite the odds.

The day finally passed and when Davey and I returned home around nine-thirty Uncle Alec told us that Aunt Jean had gone to bed already.

"She's been out of sorts this last few weeks," he said. "You know, up tight about the anniversary of your disappearance and return. She took one of those sleeping pills the doctor gave her. Quite surprised me, she did. Said everything was fine. That nothing could happen. Do you lads need anything else? 'Cause if not, I'll get to bed soon too. I'm stocktaking tomorrow."

We said goodnight and went to our room.

"Two years ago, Davey, how did you sneak out?" I said.

He laughed. "Easy. Out the window and you can drop onto the back shed roof. Then off that into the lane."

"Right, we wait until about quarter to eleven before we move."

The streets were quiet when we started out for the gym, but Davey and I stuck to the shadows and faded into darkened doorways when we saw anyone. The last thing I wanted was to be picked up now.

Davey laughed. "This is just like dodging the night watch. Remember, Pete? Going to the meeting that night when Keith was a prisoner in the castle?"

I shivered.

Yes, I remembered. Would we soon be back in the past? In the time of the Duke?

"Peter," the Duke said, "do you have a plan? How do we avoid the guards? You certainly avoided the watch I had set that night. The night you killed me."

222

Forty Six

Davey was like an overwound clockspring.

"How can you and Pete be so calm? I don't know. I feel sick."

"Who's calm?" Mike said. "I haven't felt so excited since Hunt Day last year. Will anything happen? You're right, Davey. Pete's sitting there like a bleeding Buddha."

With a start, I blinked, then smiled.

"If you two think you're excited, you should feel what it's like with our Duke in your head. He's driving me nuts. I can't get a thought in edgewise."

We sat silent, each lost in his own thoughts, till Mr Buchanan and Alf appeared, followed almost immediately by Charlie and the Duke.

"It won't be long till midnight, boys," Mr Buchanan said. "What's your plan, Peter?"

"That depends on Uncle Gerry's report," I said and turned to the Duke.

"As you know, gentlemen, I offered to supplement Inspector Cameron's patrols. His budget was so thin, he'd have had problems covering the whole perimeter." The Duke smiled. "So I've beefed up his force with some outside security. I know exactly where each man is and how far his walk takes him."

"Are they briefed to let us past?"

"No, Davey, they are not. They are honest, and not very intelligent men. Hand picked. Their employer will have indicated they are to patrol the perimeter fence all night to prevent teenage vandals or pranksters from entering the wood; nothing heroic, nothing all that serious either. The mere knowledge of their presence, their very obvious presence, should be enough."

He placed a plan on the table.

"The red crosses are Cameron's men. The black ones are mine. The lines vertical to the fence mark the end of each man's walk."

"Do they have walkie-talkies?"

"About every fourth man does."

"This stretch here," I pointed, "where the stream from the wood goes under the road. The fence runs along the edge of the pavement, doesn't it?"

"Yes, but Cameron thought of that one. He had the shore end of the culvert closed with a grill."

Deep in thought, I studied the chart.

"Before we do anything else," the Duke said, "Davey, fetch the big carton from the hall."

"Why me?"

"Because you need the exercise," we chorused and laughed.

"These are as authentic as I could manage," the Duke said. "They shouldn't create a stir beyond establishing you as gentlemen of quality."

The box contained clothing very similar to what we remembered our duke and his courtiers had worn.

We stripped and dressed in the new clothes.

"Before you put on your overshirts, fetch the second box," the Duke said.

"Chain mail shirts," Davey said. "Great."

"They're marked with your initials." The Duke pointed. "I wanted them to fit properly. They're authentic for the period, although they might not have reached the island yet. They will protect you against knife thrusts and most sword thrusts, but they will not stop a well-shot arrow or crossbow quarrel."

Fully dressed, we laughed.

"Boy, the Lords of Möbius indeed," Mike said.

"A final touch. Alf."

The Duke gestured and Alf opened a long flat box. He examined the contents closely.

"This one's yours, Davey."

He handed Davey a broad leather belt, then a sword belt.

Davey adjusted his belts while the Duke gave Mike and me similar belts.

"Now to complete the picture, a sword and dagger each."

The Duke cleared his throat, and we all turned to him.

"These are well balanced weapons, sharp, Davey. They are of better steel than was available to Duke William, but without a metallurgical chemist no one there will know. It's your one edge, no pun intended. To people there, they will simply be wondrously strong and sharp blades."

"There's something engraved on mine," Davey said.

"Yes, your Möbius Loop is engraved on each blade with your own initial in the centre of the loop. Look on the other side, down the spine groove."

"Davey, Master of the Demon Skin, of Möbius," Davey read. "Great."

"Michael, Warrior Smith, of Möbius."

"Peter, Navigator, Lord of Möbius."

We stood silent, examining the swords and daggers.

"Kneel, boys," Charlie said. "Hold out your swords before you like crosses."

Holding his hand up, Charlie said something in Latin to which I made a response before I crossed myself and stood.

"Oh, and these."

The Duke handed us each a leather belt pouch.

"There's enough gold, in coin current in London and France, for each of you to live in the style of minor lords for several years. You have somewhat more, Peter."

We started to thank him, and he said: "As I'm sure Murdoch and Charlie can tell you, it's pure selfish self-interest to protect the *status quo* here."

"Charlie," I said, "I would like you to keep this. It's the Abbot's stole that came back with me from the monastery. I had it vacuum sealed in glass, so it wouldn't go to dust the way our tunics did."

"I shall keep it for you, Pete, till you come for it."

"Back to business then," Mr Buchanan said. "I'll have your watches. What's the plan, Peter?"

 **Forty Seven**

The milk delivery float drove slowly along the promenade road and cruised to a standstill where the stream from the wood went under the road.

"You can't park there. I'm sorry, not tonight."

The security guard stepped forward, then recognised the Duke. "Your Grace. Can I help you?"

"No, I thought some tea might go down well. It's a cool night. There's an urn and cups on the back flap. Call the two lads in on either side for a cuppa. They can see their walks if they go to the other side of the road."

The guard shouted and both flank guards came in.

"Smoke if you wish, gentlemen. If we stand over here," the Duke walked across the road to the seafront railing, "we can see both directions on either side of the van."

They stood, the Duke and one guard leaning on the railing, while the other two dutifully peered in opposite directions along the promenade. Suddenly from below them came a clanking noise and a muffled oath.

"What's that?" the Duke said, loudly.

"Someone's at the culvert grill," the centre guard said. "Quick, you two, down to the beach and catch them."

Both ran in opposite directions while the centre guard shone his torch down, but couldn't see past the overhang.

"Let's split," said a voice, and three youths broke cover and ran off along the beach.

Davey, Mike, Alf, and I waited, crouched, in the milk float. We heard the footsteps cross to the other side of the road, and quietly slid out of the vehicle to the fence and dropped prone. Alf snipped with the bolt shears when he heard the shouts. The bottom of the fence moved far enough away from the pavement edge to allow us to roll through and down into the hollow where the stream entered the culvert.

Scrabbling furiously, Davey barely managed to stop short of the stream. Then he was hit from behind, and shot feet first into the stream after all.

"My new boots. You clumsy oaf."

"Sorry, lad. I meant to catch the edge of the culvert, but I missed," Alf's voice said out of the darkness.

"Alf. What are you doing here?" I said. "You were only to see us through."

"Fat chance, and have One Ear haunt me for the rest of time?" Alf said. "Where's my parcel with my clothes and sword? I had it when I rolled under the fence." He looked around. "What happened to the lights?"

We peered around. The orange glow of the sodium lights had gone. There was no fence, and where the culvert should have been, the stream ran freely down a gentle slope, and we could hear the splash on rock of a small waterfall falling over the low cliff to the beach.

"We're back," I said.

The End

Here's an exclusive preview of Hugh McCracken's
'Masters of the Hunt'.
The third in the series of thrilling time-slip books.

Chapter 1

"Hasn't changed much in a year has it?" I said.

"But it sure went downhill in seven centuries," Alf replied, looking round him at the virgin woods.

"Well, we're back," Mike said. "The grove, Pete?"

"I thought you lead in the woods, Mike." Davey's voice coming out of the darkness had a hard edge to it.

"Stow it, Davey," Mike hissed. "Pete's in charge now. All the way. We agreed."

"Move out. It's time," I told them. "Hunt status."

We trekked quietly through the woods towards the clearing with which we were all familiar. I dropped to my knees and the others immediately followed my example. At my hand signal Mike and Davey vanished into the shadows on either side to reconnoitre.

God, I thought, I'm glad the Major made us learn sign language and practice till we were fluent and even develop some special signs of our own.

Davey and Mike reappeared, shadows suddenly solidifying, eyes fully adjusted to the dark now there was quite enough light for us to see each other clearly.

"Friends at the clearing," Mike signed. "Armed men, mercenaries by the look of them, forming a cordon that way." He waved to my right.

Davey nodded and opened his mouth to speak but stopped short at the sharp chopping motion of my right hand.

"Same on the left," he signed. "A sloppy lot. They're all looking into the clearing at the Friends of the Rowan. If they're supposed to be stopping us, they're looking in the wrong direction."

"How many and how armed?"

"Four I saw. Short swords, no bows or crossbows," Mike signed. "Possibly more on the far side of the clearing. Should I check?"

"No." I shook my head and looked questioningly at Davey.

"Three well spaced out. One had a pike." Davey signed. "I don't think they can see each other from their stations."

"So if we take one out we could slip through?"

At Davey's nod I looked at Alf, who grinned.

"No unnecessary killing. Davey, lead Alf to the centre man. Alf, you take him. Mike next, then me. Move."

We moved slowly, soundless as shadows. There was a small sound out of the dark. Davey reappeared and signalled: "Clear."

Inside the cordon we kept low in the underbrush as I led us round the clearing to where I wanted us to appear. Positioned to my satisfaction I signed to the others to stand.

When we stood and stepped forward onto a small knoll at the edge of the clearing, we were clearly visible in the bright starlight.

"They've come!"

"By the Rowan, it's true then, The Masters."

"*Corpus Dominus*, it is true!"

Voices sounded all through the group gathered there. Some jubilant, some incredulous, some fearful.

"We are not spirits or apparitions, good friends. Friends of the Rowan and of Möbius. We are here in the solid flesh as before – as friends. Peter of Möbius and his brothers."

"Soldiers! Soldiers all around the Grove," a voice shouted.

At that, another more mature voice sounded above the hubbub. "Surrender in the name of the Lord Henry, Duke of this Island and the Lands Beyond. Those who do not resist will not be harmed. Seize the four strangers."

"Fall back, Friends," I shouted. "No one need be harmed. Soldiers, these people are unarmed and are merely come to greet us. We are who you were sent to stop. If you have the stomach for it, come try our mettle."

"Yield in the name of the Duke Henry."

"My ward sent you to arrest us? Be sensible. Sergeant, or Captain, put up your weapons. You must know who and what I am."

The Friends had pulled back and were now watching as the armed men closed in a semi-circle in front of my group. Some soldiers stood rather uncertainly facing the Friends. The under-brush behind us was dense — thick with brambles for at least nine or ten feet. We couldn't be jumped from the rear.

I glanced over my shoulder and the leader of the mercenaries grinned and shouted: "Now, Seize them."

Some of his men jumped forward. Two fell almost at once and the others backed off, a little wary now. When they advanced this time, the stance was that of fighting men facing other trained warriors. I picked out the leader and engaged him.

The man's initial expression of contempt rapidly changed as I easily deflected his first blows and pressed him hard. Dagger in my left hand and sword in my right, I advanced relentlessly. When the man stumbled slightly on the uneven ground I pounced. My adversary recovered and we stood, the man's sword blade locked in the angle between my sword and dagger, our bodies touching. We pushed, but neither moved. I jerked my knee hard up into the man's groin. It was not enough to knock him down, but the surprise and the pain made him slacken his grip and I disarmed him, pushing him down onto his back.

My sword point pressed at his throat, the man looked up, resignation in his eyes.

"Yield!" I said. "This is not your fight. Call on your men to lay down their arms. Yield with honour. No one else need die."

"Yield men. We signed on for an easy tour as personal guards, not for a war. Yield."

"I'll not yield to a bloody boy," one shouted.

Davey slashed his sword across the man's midriff and shouted: "Then die, fool."

The others lowered their weapons and stepped back. I pulled my opponent to his feet and he bowed.

"To whom do I yield my command, Master?"

"To Peter of Möbius, Lawful Guardian of the Infant Duke Henry, Protector of his rights."

"Hugh, lately of Chester, Captain of this band. Lately in the employ of Roland of Guisse, *soi-disant* guardian of the Infant Duke Henry.

"Do you give me your parole and that of your company, Captain?"

"Willingly, My Lord," he said. "You are not by any chance hiring?"

"You would change employers so readily, Captain?" I said. "Not the best of recommendations."

With a grin and a shrug Hugh said: "Having been defeated and given you our parole we are of little further use to Master Roland, and knowing him, he is unlikely to wish to pay even for this night's work."

"Why would you sign on with me, Captain?"

"I have survived and thrived as a mercenary, this long, by having a nose for the winning side. There is no profit in losing. I smell a winning side, My Lord."

"You speak for your men?"

"In my parole only. May I consult?"

The mercenaries withdrew to one side to discuss the matter, and Alf and I looked at the fallen.

We approached the mercenaries and I said: "You have two dead – "

Alf cleared his throat and I looked at him questioningly.

"Three, My Lord," Alf said. "The first sentry …"

I nodded, but felt my face flush. I had said no unnecessary killing.

"Three then, and three wounded. The Friends will take care of two of them."

"And the third, My Lord," Hugh said.

I led them to where a man lay writhing, desperately trying to stuff pulsating blue-black tubing into a gaping mouth in his midriff.

"Phew, what's that smell?" Davey asked.

"Bowel gas," Captain Hugh said. "I've smelt it before when a man was bowel slashed. There's nothing to be done."

"And three days to die in agony," Alf said.

"Eyes," I said. Davey, Mike, and Alf looked at me and I signed rapidly. Each of the others signed in turn, but Davey looked decidedly green.

"We have no priest," I muttered, kneeling beside the wounded man. "When I say the act of contrition, just nod."

At the man's nod, I made the sign of the cross on his forehead and said: "*In nomen Patri, Filus, et spiriti Sancti, Absolvo te.*"

The man visibly relaxed. I held his head gently while Alf cut his throat.

To be continued in Hugh McCracken's
'Masters of the Hunt'

Printed in the United Kingdom by
Lightning Source UK Ltd., Milton Keynes
137230UK00001B/70/A